Never Fear,
MEENA'S HERE!

Also by Karla Manternach

Meena Meets Her Match

The Meena Zee Books

Never Fear,
MEENA'S
HERE!

By Karla Manternach
Illustrated by Mina Price

Simon & Schuster Books for Young Readers
New York   London   Toronto   Sydney   New Delhi

SIMON & SCHUSTER BOOKS FOR YOUNG READERS
An imprint of Simon & Schuster Children's Publishing Division
1230 Avenue of the Americas, New York, New York 10020
This book is a work of fiction. Any references to historical events,
real people, or real places are used fictitiously. Other names, characters, places,
and events are products of the author's imagination, and any resemblance to actual
events or places or persons, living or dead, is entirely coincidental.
Text © 2020 by Karla Manternach
Illustrations © 2020 by Mina Price
Cover design by Tom Daly © 2020 by Simon & Schuster, Inc.
All rights reserved, including the right of reproduction in whole or in part in any form.
SIMON & SCHUSTER BOOKS FOR YOUNG READERS
and related marks are trademarks of Simon & Schuster, Inc.
For information about special discounts for bulk purchases, please contact Simon & Schuster
Special Sales at 1-866-506-1949 or business@simonandschuster.com.
The Simon & Schuster Speakers Bureau can bring authors to your live event.
For more information or to book an event, contact the Simon & Schuster Speakers Bureau
at 1-866-248-3049 or visit our website at www.simonspeakers.com.
Also available in a Simon & Schuster Books for Young Readers hardcover edition
Interior design by Tom Daly
The text for this book was set in Excelsior LT.
The illustrations for this book were rendered digitally.
Manufactured in the United States of America
0221 OFF
First Simon & Schuster Books for Young Readers paperback edition March 2021
2 4 6 8 10 9 7 5 3 1
The Library of Congress has cataloged the hardcover edition as follows:
Names: Manternach, Karla, author.
Title: Never fear, Meena's here! / Karla Manternach.
Other titles: Never fear, Meena is here!
Description: First edition. | New York : Simon & Schuster Books for Young Readers, [2020]
Sequel to: Meena meets her match. | Summary: When third-grader Meena starts
to believe she has superpowers and is protected from epileptic seizures, she
jeopardizes her relationships with her friends and younger sister.
Identifiers: LCCN 2019006133 | ISBN 9781534428201 (hardcover : alk. paper)
ISBN 9781534428218 (paperback) | ISBN 9781534428225 (eBook)
Subjects: | CYAC: Superheroes—Fiction. | Sisters—Fiction. | Friendship—Fiction.
Epilepsy—Fiction.
Classification: LCC PZ7.1.M368 Ne 2020 | DDC [Fic]—dc23
LC record available at https://lccn.loc.gov/2019006133

For Mara and Amelia—again, always.

I wave my hands in the air. "Save me!"

Sofía is yelling too.

We're sitting on scooters in the middle of the gym, crammed together with the whole class on a crumbling island. The rest of the floor is a lake of fire. Pedro runs toward us from one wall, Lin from the other. They can each only save one person as the island breaks apart beneath us!

We all press closer to the painted line and reach out as Pedro and Lin skid to a stop. Pedro grabs Eli's hand. Lin grabs Sofía's.

Excitement surges through me as Lin pulls Sofía toward her and then pushes her to safety. As soon as they tag the padded wall, Sofía jumps off her scooter, and they both sprint back toward us. Behind me, Pedro and Eli run back for two more boys.

"Come on! Come on!" everyone shouts. As soon as Sofía saves me, I can help the girls win!

I wheel myself right up to the line.

Sneakers smack against the gym floor and squeak to a stop right in front of us. I strain my hand toward Sofía. She reaches through the tangle of arms—

—and saves Nora!

"No," I cry. "Pick me!"

But she's turning away, black hair flying as she pushes Nora toward the wall. I want to kick my heels and scoot after them, over the fiery lake and onto the shore.

Time is almost up! My stomach clenches as

both teams tag the wall and leave their scooters behind. Now four kids are running from each side. The boys get here first, grab hold of their team-mates, and drag them out of the circle.

The girls reach us. "Sofía, *please*," I shout, stretching my hand as far as it will go.

She locks eyes with me, grabs my hand, and pulls me out.

Yes!

I grip the handles and lift my feet up off the floor. "Hurry," I yell. "Hurry!"

Sofía spins me around and starts pushing. I'm flying over the lake now, her hands pressing against my back, my hair whipping around me. We're closing the gap. We're nearly to shore. We're going to make it!

Tweet!

Mrs. D blares her whistle, and the boys erupt into cheers. Sofía lets go of my shoulders, and my scooter glides to a stop a few feet from the wall. I feel my whole body deflating as the boys give each other high fives. I turn to Sofía in disbelief. "Why didn't you save me?" I ask.

She's panting, hands on her knees, yellow flower headband askew. "I did."

"You saved Nora first."

Sofía stands up straight. "She was closer. Didn't you want to win?"

I thump my heel against the floor. "I don't care about winning."

She raises her eyebrows at me.

"Okay, I care a little," I say. "But what's the point of being best friends if we don't pick each other first? I didn't even get a chance to save anybody."

Sofía pushes her scooter over to me. "Want a ride to the equipment closet?"

I cross my arms and scowl. "No."

She crosses her arms back at me and smirks.

I glance over at Mrs. D, twirling her whistle while everybody gets into line, and my mouth turns up. "Yeah, okay."

I flop over, chest on one scooter, stomach on the other, knees bent. Sofía grabs my feet and starts to push. Pretty soon she's running, and the floor is whizzing by. I spread my arms and feel like I'm flying, my best friend at my back, giving me one last push that sends me spinning before—

Tweet! "Girls! Bottoms on the scooters!"

We have to cover our mouths to keep from laughing when we line up with everyone else, first because Mrs. D said "bottoms," and second because we're not supposed to be happy about breaking the rules, even if we are.

I'm last in line as we head for our cubbies. My feet are hot, so I take off my socks and shoes while nobody is looking and walk barefoot down the hall. Just a few more minutes until the weekend! Sofía and I stayed in for lunch recess today, so I'm extra itchy to get out of here. I'm not a huge fan of practicing handwriting while she catches up on math, but I *am* a big fan of Sofía, so I guess it's okay. The good news is that all the extra work has been making my handwriting *awesome*.

The bad news is that Mrs. D told me today to erase all the extra swirls.

I wish she'd let me write my own way. Back in kindergarten, the teacher used to let us practice letters with colored pencils. He loved everything I wrote, even though I couldn't spell. And when I made up my own words at our spring concert, he just shook his head and laughed.

Mrs. D doesn't let me do any of that stuff. Today I even got in trouble in art class.

Art class!

We were supposed to copy a painting of a panda bear holding a bamboo stalk. "You have total freedom," she said. "You can make the stalk longer or leafier than the picture. You can make the bear fatter or taller."

I painted myself holding a magic wand instead. It's not my fault Mrs. D doesn't know what "total freedom" is!

It seems like I have to spend every minute at

school acting like all the other kids. I do the same worksheets as everyone else and get the same answers. I play the same games and sing the same songs.

But I don't want to be like everyone else. I want to be me—the one and only Meena Zee!

At least I'm Sofía's one and only. This afternoon, I finally get her all to myself. We'll make popcorn and do projects in my workshop. Maybe we'll make our new friendship bracelets too—if she ever finishes packing up, that is.

"Did you remember your social studies homework?" she asks, pulling folders out of her cubby.

"Oh, yeah. Thanks." I cram it into my bag. "Did you pack up your scented markers?"

"Right!" She grabs them and nestles them into the front pouch of her backpack. She starts checking her assignment notebook next, running her finger slowly down the page.

I zip up my bag, stuff my socks in my pocket, and cram my feet into my shoes again. Other kids are already leaving. I stand and bounce from foot to foot. Sofía is very thorough, so this could take a while.

"You want to meet outside?" she asks, glancing up at me.

"I don't mind waiting for you."

She chuckles. "Yes, you do. It's okay. I'll be out in a minute."

I give her a relieved smile. "Okay," I say, then bound down the hall and burst through the exit.

I take a deep breath of sunshine and blow the stuffy school air out of my lungs. In the flower beds along the building, green stems are starting to poke through the dirt. All around me, kids skip away from school. Cars pull up in a single-file line. The bus sits rumbling at the end of the sidewalk, puffing out exhaust.

It smells like freedom.

I check the ground for interesting trash. There's not much since yesterday—just a broken stub of pencil and the straw from a juice box. Someone did drop a sock, though.

Hang on.

I feel the breeze on my bare ankles and check my pockets. That might be mine.

When I bend over to scoop it up, I spot something. It's small and silver. A quarter? I pounce before anyone sees it. But when I pick it up and look closer, I see a hole in the middle, not quite big enough for my pinky finger.

Huh. Usually, I can tell what things used to be before someone got rid of them, but I don't know what this is. It's round and perfectly smooth, like a coin from someplace so ancient that they didn't use words yet. When you turn it over, the silver has a rainbow sheen.

I rub my thumb along the edge. Whatever it is, I can turn it into something cool. Maybe I'll pretend it's a monocle. Or maybe I can stick it in one of the gumball machines at the hardware store and get something out for *free*.

I check over my shoulder for Sofía, then tap my foot, watching cars pull away from the curb. Lin climbs into her mom's pickup truck. A fifth grader gets in the front seat of his babysitter's car. The Taylor twins pile into the back seat of their van. Their dad turns all the way around to help one of them with a seat belt. A first grader starts to walk in front of them, her curly black hair sproinging out of pigtails.

She's not supposed to cross here. Mrs. Nelson is nearby, waving kids through the crosswalk in a bright orange vest.

The girl is directly in front of the twins' van when her lunch box pops open. Plastic containers hit the pavement. She stops and scoops them up. I'm about to go over and help her when her water bottle rolls under the van. Through the windshield, I see Mr. Taylor turn back around in his seat.

"Hey," I say to the girl, but she doesn't look up, and I don't know her name.

Mr. Taylor glances over his shoulder.

"Hey!" I say a bit louder. She's down on one knee now, reaching under the van.

Mr. Taylor puts a hand on the steering wheel.

He sees her, right?

The van inches forward.

I gasp. He doesn't see her!

"Stop!" I yell. I leap off the curb and wave my arms. When Mr. Taylor slams on the brakes, the van jerks to a stop. I suck in a quick breath.

Mr. Taylor throws open his door. "Are you okay?" he asks, climbing out.

I lower my arms, my heart pounding.

"What on earth are you doing?" he demands.

"There's a kid in front of you." I point. "Look!"

The girl stands up, stuffs the containers into her lunch box, and latches it shut. Then she skips away, clueless.

Mr. Taylor watches her, his face going white. The twins lean forward in the back seat to look at me. Car doors open in the loading line, and parents step out and stare.

"What's going on?" Sofía asks, coming up beside me.

"Meena saved that kid's life!" I turn and see Aiden from our class running up.

He points across the parking lot. A frantic-looking lady has the first-grade girl by the shoulders, saying something right into her face. She gives the girl a little shake, then hugs her, hard.

The girl looks right at me over the lady's shoulder, eyes wide.

"Mr. Taylor almost ran that girl over," Aiden cries.

I shoot him a look.

"Seriously, she could have *died*," he says, beaming.

I glance at Mr. Taylor, who takes out a hankie and wipes it across his forehead. "You weren't driving that fast," I say.

"But if anything had happened . . ." His voice trails off. He looks woozy, like he just bit into a chicken tender and found out it was fried fish instead.

"It wasn't your fault," I say, giving his sleeve a tug. "She practically crawled under your van."

He nods, grabbing a fistful of his hair. Behind him, one of the twins rolls down a window. "Are we going?"

Mr. Taylor straightens. He lets go of his hair and rakes his fingers through it a few times. "Your name is Meena?" he asks. I nod. He takes my hand and shakes it, smiling weakly. "Thank you, Meena. How does it feel to be a hero?"

I pull away. "I'm not a hero. Anybody would have done that."

"But you're the only one who did."

Mr. Taylor gets back into his van. He checks all around him once, twice, three times before he pulls away from the curb. The twins watch me out the rear window until they turn the corner, out of sight.

"What was *that* all about?" Sofía asks.

I don't answer, because right then I feel something smooth and round in my other hand again.

I stare down at the metal ring—the one I picked up right before I saved that girl.

What is this thing?

I squeeze it tight, Mr. Taylor's words echoing in my ears: *a hero.*

Me?

My chest fills up like a balloon. I think I could get used to that.

2

We're about a block from school when I turn to look back, still dazed. The parking lot is almost empty. Only a few kids are standing by the building, waiting for their rides. "Do you think I really saved that girl's life?" I ask.

"I don't know," Sofía says.

We turn toward home again and walk in silence. Every once in a while, I wander over to the curb to pick up a flattened soda can or a stretchy scrap of road tar. "I didn't even think about it," I say finally. "It was almost like . . ." I scratch the back of my neck. "You know how you yank your hand away when you touch something hot? Before it actually hurts?"

"Yeah," Sofía says.

"It was like that. I didn't *decide* to jump in front of that van. I just did it." I lower my voice. "It was almost like something made me."

Sofía squints at me. "Something . . . like what?"

"Right before it happened . . ." I check over my

shoulder and huddle close to her. "I found this." I open my hand.

Sofía blinks down at the metal ring. "What is it?"

"I don't know."

She leans in closer. "It looks like a quarter with a hole in it."

"Look, though," I say. "There's nothing on it."

"Maybe it came off an earring?" She picks it up and turns it over. "There aren't any hooks or anything." She hands it back. "What do you think it is?"

"Well . . ." I swallow, not wanting to sound crazy. "You know how Superman didn't have powers until he came to earth?"

"Yeah," Sofía says slowly.

"And how Spider-Man was a regular guy until he got bit by that weird lab spider?" She nods. I hold up the ring, looking right at her. "What if this activates my powers?" I whisper.

Sofía's eyebrows shoot up. "Are you serious?"

"Well, who knows where it came from or what it can do?" I say. "Maybe *anybody* who picked it up would have gotten activated. What if it just happened to be me?" I grab her wrist. "What if I found it just in time to *save that girl's life*?"

Sofía opens her mouth like she's going to say something, but then she moves her jaw back and forth instead, the way she does when she's trying to figure out a division problem.

I let my hands fall to my sides. "You don't think so?" I say.

"I just . . ." She bites her lip. "You really think that thing turned you into a superhero?"

I straighten at the word.

That's even better than a regular hero!

I tuck the ring into my pocket. "I think I want to find out."

Mom turns away from her computer and stares at me. "You jumped in front of a van?"

I shrug. "It wasn't going very fast."

She takes off her glasses and rubs her eyes. "Meena . . ."

"What? You never told me I couldn't."

"I actually have to say that out loud?" She puts her hands on my arms and peers hard at me. "No more throwing yourself at moving vehicles."

"Aw . . ."

"Got it?"

My shoulders slump. "Yeah, I got it."

Her face relaxes. "But I'm glad everybody's okay."

I kiss her on the cheek. "Can we make popcorn?"

"Of course."

I bounce over to the cabinet and wink at Sofía. She isn't supposed to eat popcorn because of her braces, but Mom doesn't know that. "What flavor do you want?" I ask. "Low-fat or low-sodium?"

She grins. "Low-fat."

"Sofíaaaaaaaaa!" Rosie runs in from the living room. She drops Pink Pony and hurls herself at Sofía, who catches her with an *oomph*.

"How was morning kindergarten, Rosie Posey?" Sofía doesn't have a sister, so she actually likes talking to mine.

"A leprechaun came to our room," Rosie says. "He left footprints on the board when we weren't there and spilled green glitter all over the floor!" She giggles. "He's naughty."

"Hey, Rosie," I say. "Do you know what popcorn sounds like when it's ready?"

She slides down the front of Sofía and lands on her feet. "Pop!" She pauses. She bobs her head as she counts in her head. "Pop!" she says again.

"Can you bring it upstairs when it's finished?"

She does a little hop. "Okay."

"Meena can wait for it herself, honey," Mom says, clicking at her computer.

"I'll do it," Rosie says.

Mom looks at me over the top of her glasses.

"What?" I say, tugging on one of Rosie's pigtails. "She loves doing me favors. It makes her happy."

"It would make her happier to hang out with you."

"We'll see." I press start on the microwave and point my finger in the air. "To the workshop!"

"Aren't you going to tell your mom about the ring?" she asks when we get upstairs.

I close the door behind us. "Are you crazy? You heard what she said about jumping in front of cars. She never lets me do anything! Besides" — I pick up my stuffed zebra from where I left him looking out the window this morning — "if I *am* a superhero, only one person can know my secret identity, and that's already you." I give Raymond a squeeze. "Well, you and Raymond, but he won't tell, right?"

I make him cross his heart with his hoof.

"So, what do you think I should wear?" I toss Raymond up in the air to give him a thrill, since he hasn't had anything to do all day — that we know of.

Sofía catches him and nuzzles his neck. "Wear for what?"

"I need an outfit if I'm a superhero, right?"

She tosses him back. "I don't think that's what it's called."

"A costume?" I make Raymond do a double flip, his rainbow stripes a blur of color.

Sofía catches him. "A suit, I think."

"Right!" My tie-dyed hoodie is on the floor, so I pull it on, put my hands on my hips, and thrust my chest out. "How do I look?"

"Same as always."

"Okay, but picture it with a cape. And something to cover my face. A mask, maybe. Or, no, a helmet! Definitely a helmet."

"Doesn't matter. You wear that all the time. Everybody will know it's you."

She has a point. "I just feel like I should match the Rainbow Ring."

That's when I get an Inspiration.

"Or maybe it came looking like this so it could match *me*," I whisper.

I dive through my supply bins and rummage until I find—there! I dig out my old sneakers and pull off one of the rainbow laces. It's a little frayed at the ends, but I slide the Rainbow Ring onto it, tie it around my neck, and tuck it into my shirt. I don't want it out where everyone can see it, in case someone lost it and is missing their powers.

I hear Rosie thumping up the stairs and open the door. She's cradling a big bowl of popcorn. "Thanks, squirt," I say, lifting it out of her hands.

She pokes her head in. "What are you doing?"

"Making bracelets."

"Can I make one?"

"They're not for sisters. They're for friends."

Her face falls. "I'm your friend."

"Bye, Rosie." I give her enough of a push to get her back into the hall and close the door.

When I turn around, Sofía is frowning at me.

"What?" I say. "I was nice about it."

"I don't mind if she hangs out with us," she says. "Why can't she come in?"

"I see Rosie every day."

"I don't."

I sigh and set down the bowl. "You don't have to share a room with her either. Or let her tag along when you're working on projects. She's everywhere!"

Sofía crosses her arms right over the top of Raymond, which makes him look like he's choking. "That doesn't sound so bad."

But I don't want Rosie around. Not this time. Sofía and I went more than a month without talking to each other over the winter, and even though we made up weeks ago, I still feel like we have catching up to do. Ever since then, sometimes I feel like just another one of her friends—like when Pedro makes a joke in Spanish that only she understands, or she invites Maddy and Nora to stay in for recess with us. If it were up to her, everybody would always be included. Even boys who fold their eyelids inside out and kid sisters. I don't even have a bracelet to show the world I'm special—her *best* friend. The one and only.

I pry Raymond gently out of her grip and smooth his rainbow-striped mane. "Can't we just finish our bracelets?" I ask. "I haven't had you to myself all week."

Sofía's face softens into half a smile. When she picks up the jar of beads we've been saving, I let out a breath and plop down on the floor.

We dump out all the beads and cut pieces of plastic string. Up until now, we haven't been able to agree on how our bracelets should look. I want rainbow colors, but Sofía wants pastels. "So, what's it gonna be?" I ask.

She grabs a handful of popcorn and chews thoughtfully. "Let's just make them however we want," she says. "We don't match. Our bracelets shouldn't have to either."

I guess that's true. Maybe it doesn't matter what they look like, so long as everybody knows what they mean.

Because friendship bracelets work the same way as calling the top bunk or sticking your finger in a cupcake so no one else takes it.

They let everybody know what belongs to you.

At least now we don't have to figure out who gets the only yellow bead. I pick it out of the pile and thread it onto my string. I want it to look like a diamond with all the other colors of the rainbow circling it. As I thread more beads together, I start thinking about the Rainbow Ring, and pretty soon I'm picturing the superhero movie poster they'll make for me someday. I can see it perfectly: a rainbow burst, radiating across the page. Right in the center is me, wearing—

I stop working and stare out the window. I'm

trying so hard to imagine my suit that I only sort of hear Sofía when she says, "Meena?"

She snaps her fingers in my face.

I blink. "What?"

"Sorry," she says, looking relieved. "Just making sure you're still here."

I scowl and bend over my bracelet again. Sofía was the first one to notice that I have mini seizures. She says when I space out, it looks like I'm daydreaming, except I don't remember it afterward. All I know is that time jumps forward, and someone is usually snapping in my face.

That part is pretty annoying.

"What do you think," I ask, "tights or leggings?"

"For what?"

"My supersuit."

"Oh. Leggings, I guess."

"That's what I thought." I thread a few purple beads onto each side of the string. "We should talk about your suit too."

"Why would I need a suit?"

"So you can be my sidekick."

Sofía stops threading beads and gapes at me. "I'm not going to be your *sidekick*. Besides, we don't know if you *are* a superhero yet."

"I saved that girl, didn't I? I must have some kind of special powers."

"Special powers don't make you a hero. Even villains have those."

She's right. I put my hand on my chest and feel the outline of the Ring under my shirt. "But villains don't save people," I say slowly.

That's how I'll find out for sure if I'm a super-hero, I realize.

I need to find more people to save.

3

When I wake up on Saturday, Rosie's bed is a pile of covers next to mine. I stretch out my arm and gaze at my new bracelet in every color of the rainbow.

Then I remember.

I sit up and feel for the Ring around my neck. *Yes!* It wasn't a dream. I bolt out of bed, hurry to my workshop, and breathe on the window. Traces of my last picture reappear in the Magic Mist: a circle of fingerprints from yesterday morning, when my only wish was to make bracelets with Sofía.

Today I draw a stick figure at the center of the circle with her hands on her hips. I make a squiggly line to look like a cape flapping in the breeze, then I close my eyes and make a wish.

I want to save someone again.

I know a thing or two about superheroes. I've seen a bunch of the old cartoons with Dad. Once in a while, Mom even lets us watch one of the movies, as long as Dad covers my eyes for the good parts. So I know the first thing I need to do is get to a big city.

Because superheroes are always hanging out on top of skyscrapers.

"Anybody want to take a trip today?" I ask, bounding into the kitchen.

"Meena!" Rosie springs from the table and hugs me around my stomach like she hasn't seen me in years.

"Where to?" Mom asks, handing me a plate.

"I don't know. New York. Metropolis. Maybe Gotham?"

"Some of those places aren't even real," Dad says from the stove.

"New York isn't real?"

Dad chuckles and lifts a pancake onto his spatula. "Incoming!" He flicks his wrist, and the pancake sails through the air right at me! I leap for it and let it bounce off my chest before I catch it on my plate.

Wow! My reflexes are amazing! "Do it again," I say.

Mom clears her throat. Dad winks at me, lifts another pancake off the griddle, and walks it over. I grin and slide into my chair.

"Milk's in the fridge," Mom says.

Rosie is arranging the strawberries on her

plate into a smiley face. I nudge her with my elbow.

"Oh!" She jumps up. "I'll get it!" She runs for the fridge and lugs the gallon of milk to the counter in both arms.

"Just a second, Rosie." Mom gets up and reaches into a cupboard. While she's not looking, I flood my pancakes with syrup and scoop fruit salad into the puddles, checking to make sure I have all the colors: strawberry, orange, pineapple, kiwi, and a few purple grapes. Perfect.

I'm about take a bite when Rosie bounces over and hands me her old pink sippy cup.

"What's this for?" I ask.

"Your milk."

I thrust it back at her. "I'm not drinking out of that!"

Rosie looks hurt.

"I just thought it'd be easier than mopping up spills," Mom says.

I stab a grape. Okay, so I've been knocking over a lot of glasses lately. Sometimes I even fling cereal off my spoon without meaning to. My arms are herky and jerky in the morning. It goes with the spacing out and the whole-body-shaking seizure I had once. The doctor says I have epilepsy. You know what she *doesn't* say?

She doesn't say I have to drink out of my sister's sippy cup!

"Let me see that," Dad says. He takes the milk from Rosie and pours it into a cup for me. "Why don't we let you pick out a sport bottle?" he asks.

"Good idea," Mom says. "I'm going to the hardware store after breakfast if you want to come. I bet they have some."

I perk up at the offer. The hardware store is the perfect place to get ideas for my suit!

"We can look at paint colors for your room while we're there too," Mom says.

Holy hippo, this day just keeps getting better! My bedroom walls are this barely-there gray that Mom and Dad picked out before I was born. They thought it would be soothing, but I say painting a baby's room gray is *giving* her something to cry about.

Clearly, they hadn't met me yet.

"I know exactly what I want." I jump up from the table and gesture toward the wall. "A band of yellow down by the floor, then it fades into orange, then red and all the other colors until you get to the top, and the *whole ceiling is purple!*" Now, *that's* a room fit for a superhero. It will even match the Rainbow Ring! I start skipping around the table.

Dad holds up his hands. "Whoa there."

I stop. "What?"

"I hate to tell you this, kiddo," he says, "but it's not your turn to pick."

I stare at him. "But it's my room!"

"You have two rooms, my dear," Mom says. "Which is a little embarrassing if you think about it."

"Rosie's the one who wants to share."

"Which is why we let you have your own workshop . . . and why you got to pick bright orange for the walls, although it nearly killed me."

"So who gets to pick this time? You?"

"Your sister, of course."

Rosie looks up from popping the last strawberry into her mouth. "Me?"

"It's your room too, honey," Mom says. "Your only room."

"But she'll want pink!"

Rosie's eyes grow wide. "I can have pink?"

Mom smiles. "You can have whatever you want."

I'm still mad when we walk into the hardware store. But I'm not gonna lie: that first whiff of sawdust and garden hose . . .

It helps.

I turn and wave my hands at the automatic door, pretending that I'm the one making it swish shut. *BAM!* Next, I wiggle my feet into the prickly rubber mat, then I head to the gumball machines, turn all the cranks, and lift the little flaps, just in case.

"Did you bring any money?" I ask Rosie. Sometimes our cousin Eli gives her a couple of quarters for helping him clean cages, because Aunt Kathy actually gives him an allowance, unlike some people I know.

Rosie opens her sparkly pink purse, rifles through mini ponies and plastic gemstones, and pulls out two quarters. She spends hers on a big gumball, but I know those things are just air inside a sugary crust, so I get a bouncy ball instead.

"Can I use your phone to take pictures?" I ask Mom. "In case I get an Inspiration."

She hands it to me. "Just don't set it down anywhere. We'll be in the paint department."

I bounce my ball down the main aisle and start taking photos. If I ever do convince Mom and Dad to give me an allowance, I bet I'll blow it all here. There's a spool of chain that looks thick enough to lasso a dragon and a tool pouch that would make a perfect utility belt. I bounce from one aisle to the next, spelling "kapow" with mailbox letters, wondering if heavy-duty sandpaper would make good armor, and pointing a caulk gun at the ceiling.

But it's not long before I'm bouncing my ball toward my favorite part of the store.

Mom and Rosie are standing in front of the wall of paint samples. The sight of those little cards arranged in a rainbow waterfall warms my chest. Some of the colors blast. Others whisper. Standing there, letting each one speak for itself, feels a lot like staring at blades of grass until suddenly your eyes adjust and you see little ants running around too.

This is the only place I respect the boring colors. Here, I can see what they're made of. The whites and the grays and the beiges have more color in them than you notice at first. One is more red, another more yellow, another a little more blue.

But I still like the bright colors best of all.

Mom is already holding a couple of cards, each with five shades of the same color, darkest to lightest: a green one (celery to evergreen) and a yellow one (butter to marigold).

Rosie is holding ten different shades of pink.

I groan. A few weeks ago, Maddy brought birthday cupcakes to school. When it was finally my turn to pick, I took the orange one. But then Aiden wouldn't take the last cupcake because it was frosted pink, and so Mrs. D made me *trade*!

I should have stuck my finger in the one I wanted.

I don't know why some people think boys are allergic to pink. They act like it's a girl color, but why should it be? Why do *I* have to get stuck with watered-down, wishy-washy red? The whole thing makes me mad all the way down to my toes, and if I have to wake up every morning to pink, I'm gonna want to punch something.

"I'm going to go get some tomato seeds," Mom says. "Meena, do you want to pick out a water bottle?"

I hand back her phone. "You can do it. Anything but pink," I say. "Or white or beige or gray." When she's gone, I start running my hand over the cards, listening to the little flicks they make against my fingers.

Suddenly, I stop. My eyes zoom in on a card. My throat swells as all the other colors disappear.

You know how nature uses some colors more than others? Green grass. Blue sky. Plenty of fruits and vegetables that are yellow and orange and red.

But purple. That's a tough color to find. If you're trying to eat the rainbow, it's the hardest one to get—especially if your mom only buys dyed foods from health stores that squeeze vegetables into cereal somehow. Most of the time, you'll settle for bluish purple instead. You'll eat blueberries and grapes and plums when you can get them. When they're out of season, your mom will try to convince you that beets should count as purple, even though they juice red all over your plate.

Plus, they taste like pickled dirt.

But let's say that on those days when you can't

stand eating one more slice of eggplant, you go to bed in a room that's the very purple-blue color you're missing so you can fill up on it while you sleep.

Wouldn't you want your room to be painted that color?

I stuff my bouncy ball into my pocket and reach for the card. It's like royal blue that's been dipped in purple velvet near a fire that makes it glow. It's like staring into the sky at dusk, right when that first star blinks into view.

And it's right here, calling to me from a two-inch strip.

Maybe I can hear colors. Maybe that's one of my powers!

"Rosie," I whisper. "Look at this one."

She leans closer. "Purple?"

"It's not just purple. There's blue in it, too." I clutch the Rainbow Ring, almost swooning now. I *need* this color. "Don't you want to wake up to this?" I ask. "Isn't it the first thing you'd like to see every day?"

She takes the card.

This one, I say to myself, over and over. I squeeze my eyes shut, pushing the thought toward Rosie, wishing for her to pick it.

"See anything you like?"

My eyes snap open. Mom is standing over us with a bright orange water bottle.

I make one last silent plea: *This one!*

Rosie holds up my card. "This one," she says.

I yank my hand away from the Rainbow Ring like it's just burst into flames.

Did I make Rosie pick that color *with my mind?*

"I thought you wanted pink," Mom says.

"I want this," Rosie says. "It's pretty."

Mom's eyes flick to me, her mouth pulling into a thin line. "How about we tape the card to your wall and see how it looks? We can come back and buy the paint when you're sure."

"Okay," says Rosie. She skips down the aisle, pigtails bouncing.

Mom turns on me, hands on her hips. "What did you do?"

"I didn't do anything," I say, dazed.

But did I?

Rosie was about to pick the wrong color, and I stopped her. I *saved* her. All by myself. In the nick of time.

POW!

Mom frowns. She rubs her forehead then turns and follows Rosie down the aisle.

I trace the circle of the Rainbow Ring through my shirt.

I wonder what else this baby can do.

The rest of the weekend, I collect supplies for my supersuit. Here's what I discover:

1. I could use an umbrella that shoots lasers.
2. Hollowed-out tuna cans would make good wrist guards if they didn't go flying when you karate chop the air.
3. If you think your mom is going to spend fifty bucks on an old-fashioned trash can so you can use the lid as a shield, you must be out of your mind.

I'm still thinking about my suit at breakfast on Monday when my arm jerks and my cereal bowl goes flying. Rosie yelps. Mom jumps up and lifts her computer away from the milk. Dad tosses me a dish towel.

If there weren't all these people around, I'd try

blinking the mess away. Instead, I wipe the table dry and dab up the drips on the floor.

"Nice work, sarge," Dad says when I finish. "Miss Rosie, are you ready to go?"

She holds out the milk-soaked front of her shirt. "I'm wet."

That's when I get an Inspiration. "I could walk her to school," I say.

Rosie gasps. She hops up out of her chair. "Can she, Daddy?"

"I'm not sure we're ready to try that again," Mom says.

"Why not?" I ask. "You let me do it at the beginning of the year."

"That was before you tried to hitch a ride because Rosie was walking too slow."

I wave that off. "I was a little kid then. I know what I'm doing now."

Mom and Dad exchange a look. Rosie is bouncing on her toes, hugging herself.

"I don't know," Dad says, scratching the back of his neck. "I don't think Rosie is interested."

"I'm interested," she cries.

He smirks. "You *are*?"

"Yes!" She starts running in place.

"Because I'm not getting that."

"*Pleeeeeease*," she squeals. She squeezes her eyes shut and clasps her hands together.

"I guess we can give it a shot," Dad says.

"Woo!" Rosie thrusts her fists in the air and runs around the kitchen table. "This is going to be the best . . . walk . . . ever!"

"I'll try not to take that personally." Dad laughs. "Now go change."

Rosie zooms out of the kitchen.

"And you, Meena Zee," Mom says, standing up. "Be good to your sister."

I roll my eyes at that. "I'm always good to her."

"Except for when you leave her behind. Or hide from her. Or make her pick up soggy socks and put them in her backpack."

"I only did that once!"

"I mean it, kiddo. Rosie worships the ground you walk on. Don't take advantage of her."

"Oooh," Dad says, rubbing his hands together. "Can I give her the Spider-Man speech?"

Mom sighs. "Always with the Spider-Man speech."

Dad thrusts out his chest, fists on his hips. "With great power—"

"—comes great responsibility," I mutter. "Yeah, yeah, I know."

Rosie comes running back into the room. She slides to a stop in her socks and starts putting on her shoes.

"I'll be there to bring you home at lunchtime,

Rosie," Mom says. "Just remember to hold hands crossing the street."

"We will," I grumble, putting on my jacket.

"And remember that Rosie goes straight to the building. The kindergarteners don't wait outside with the rest of you."

"I know."

"And if anybody calls here saying you didn't report to school on time—"

"They won't, Mom! Geez. I know how to walk her."

"You're walking *with* her," Mom says, kissing us each on the cheek. "She's your sister, not a dog."

I keep my eyes peeled as I strut down the sidewalk, my shoulders back, the Rainbow Ring thumping under my shirt. It's a big job, protecting your little sister. You never know where danger lurks, or when disaster might strike.

Rosie starts running ahead. She always does that—takes off for a clean patch of snow or a new clump of dandelions.

Not today. Not on my watch. Heroes don't follow. They lead.

"Come back here," I say. "You have to stay with me."

"Dad lets me go first."

"Well, I don't. It's my job to keep you safe."

She looks around at the houses we're passing, with their painted shutters and stenciled mailboxes. "Safe from what?"

"What if a dragon swooped down and carried you away?"

She crosses her arms. "Dragons are nice."

"Maybe that's what they *want* you to think," I say. "Maybe they wait until you're all cozy and comfortable, and then *wham-o*! They grab you by the neck and carry you off to their lair."

Her eyes widen. "What would you do?"

I brush myself off. "I'd save you, obviously."

"Ha!" She slaps her hands on her thighs. "You couldn't save me from that! Mommy would have to."

"For your information, I saved a girl just last week."

"Did not."

"Did too."

"What girl?"

"Someone at school. You don't know her."

She squints at me. "From a dragon?"

I shrug. "Basically."

"Did not."

"Did too!"

I get another Inspiration then. I am on *fire* today!

"Maybe I'll let you help me next time," I say.

Rosie narrows her eyes at me. "How?"

I grab her hand to cross the street, thinking hard.

"You could do sound effects," I say. "That way I don't have to go around yelling, 'BAM!' every time I save someone."

Rosie might not make a bad sidekick, I realize. I can picture her now in a shimmery blue suit with silver boots. Maybe she'd even have wings— little wings, though, like the kind chickens have that don't actually work, because she sure can't fly if I can't.

Hang on.

I stop. Rosie takes another step, but when her hand yanks out of mine, she turns to look at me. "What?" she asks.

I stare at her. "Nothing," I say slowly. "I was just wondering . . ."

Can I fly?

My heart starts to beat faster. I don't know. I wasted the whole weekend dreaming up costumes when I should have been testing my powers!

I have to find out what else I can do. But first I have to get Rosie to school.

Maybe I can do both at once!

I gaze down the long sidewalk that leads to the main entrance. Am I faster than a speeding bullet?

Let's find out.

I grip the straps of my backpack. "Race you," I say.

I'm off like a shot, blasting past her, pumping my arms, my backpack thumping. I'm strong and fast and free, hair flying, lungs stinging. When I reach the front doors, I stop and turn around, gasping for air.

Rosie is only halfway down the walk, so I must have been *super* fast!

Then again, she's doing that little fairy run of hers, up on her toes, arms flitting at her sides. Maybe I would have beat her anyway.

So super speed? Maybe.

"Told you I'd get you here safe," I say when Rosie catches up. The aide is right inside, waiting to walk kindergarteners to their classroom.

"Rosie Posey, wait!"

Sofía runs up from behind us. I see her mom standing at the end of the long walk in her rose-garden shawl. I wave. She smiles and waves back before turning and heading the other way.

"I have something for you," Sofía says, panting. She reaches up and straightens her red flower headband.

Rosie lifts her eyebrows. "For me?"

Sofía pushes up the sleeve of her jacket. When I see the sky blue–and–lavender bracelet she made, I give my wrist a little shake, feeling my own beads click.

Then Sofía reaches under her sleeve and pulls out another bracelet.

It's pink and white, on a stretchy string that slides right over her hand.

Wait a second. . . .

"Here," Sofía says.

Rosie gasps. "You made one for *me*?"

"Sure." She slips the bracelet onto Rosie's wrist. "You're my friend too, right?"

My stomach clenches like a fist as Rosie breaks into a huge smile and slams Sofía with a hug. When she pulls back, she thrusts her wrist in my face. "Meena, did you see?"

"I saw." I jerk the door open. "Get going."

Rosie skips inside and waves at Sofía over her shoulder.

When she's gone, I let go of the door and turn on Sofía. "Why did you do that?"

She blinks at me. "I like Rosie."

"But those were *our* bracelets."

She holds up her wrist. "We still have ours."

"They're not special if everybody has one!"

Her eyebrows shoot up. "I didn't make one for everybody."

"You could have asked me first."

"Why?" She crosses her arms. "Are you saying I can't be friends with your sister?"

"I'm saying—" I smack my hands over my face.

The bracelets are supposed to be one of a kind, like our friendship is.

Or at least like it used to be.

"Look, I don't want to fight," I say finally. "Can you please just help me before the bell rings?"

"With what?"

I take a big breath and give myself a shake, letting the hurt shimmy down my arms and out the tips of my fingers. Then I lean in close and cup my hand to her ear.

"Help me figure out what my powers are."

5

Sofía and I hurry across the dewy playground, drop our backpacks, and climb into the orange tube slide. As long as the first graders are playing freeze tag, it's nice and private in here.

Which is perfect, because I don't want to get caught performing any superhuman feats.

"Let's see if I can levitate," I say. I figure that must be the first step to flying.

"Um, okay . . ." Sofía sits cross-legged at the foot of the slide.

I lie back, fold my arms across my chest, and close my eyes. I concentrate on floating into the air—a few inches to start. I breathe in and out, imagining myself getting lighter, picturing the empty space beneath me opening up. It's so clear in my mind that I'm sure I *must* be hovering.

I sit up. "So?"

Sofía shakes her head. "Nope."

"I'm sure I felt myself lifting a little bit."

She climbs out, kneels on the ground, and

rests her chin on the slide. "Try again."

I close my eyes and take long, deep breaths. I imagine huge rubber bands stretched around the back of me, tightening, pulling me upward. My back starts to tingle.

"There!" I sit up again. "Did you see it?"

She grimaces. "Sorry."

"But I felt it!" I frown. "I *thought* I did."

"Maybe it's not one of your powers," Sofía says, climbing back in.

"Or maybe I need more practice."

"Can we go play four square now?"

"Not yet. I want to check out my brain powers too." I tell her about using mind control on Rosie over the weekend. "Do you think I can do anything else?"

"Like what?"

"Maybe I can read minds." I get a little jolt of excitement. "Let's see."

"Okay." Sofía closes her eyes. "What number am I thinking of?"

I concentrate as hard as I can, squeezing my eyes shut and breathing in the plasticky smell of the slide. "Eighty-one."

"No, twenty-seven."

"Don't *tell* me. Let me figure it out. Try again." I wait until her eyes are closed, then stare deep into my brain. "Thirty-four."

"Close."

"Thirty-five."

"Keep going."

"Thirty-six?" I open one eye. She's nodding now. "Thirty-seven? Thirty-eight?"

"Yes!" Her eyes snap open.

I let out a breath. "I knew I could do it! Think of something else. Not a number this time."

I cover my eyes and sit still, breathing in and out. Hands slap the monkey bars nearby. Feet trample the soccer field in the distance.

"Anything?" Sofía asks.

I get an image of a little girl skipping through the woods with a basket on her arm. "Are you think-ing about Little Red Riding Hood? Because that's what popped into my head."

"Nope. I was picturing Pedro wrapped in toi-let paper like a mummy."

"Oh." I open my eyes. "That was way off."

"Hey!" Eli sticks his head into the top of the slide.

"Come on in," Sofía says.

I give her a side eye. "Actually, we're a little busy in here."

Eli climbs in anyway. "Just tell me what this sounds like." He starts doing this weird, chugging thing with his mouth, all teeth and lips, spit flying everywhere.

I cover my face with my hands. "Eli!"

Sofía is laughing. "Is that a helicopter?"

He stops chugging and beams at us. "I'm getting it ready to show my brother."

I lower my arms. "Riley's coming?" I ask. "When?"

"This weekend. He has a week off for spring break. Mom says we should have the whole family over so you and Rosie can see him too." He lights up. "Maybe I'll do a sound-effects concert for everyone!"

I groan.

"Want to see me do a sprinkler?" Eli asks.

"Yeah," Sofía says.

I feel a twinge of jealousy. "But we were in the middle of something," I say, nudging her with my knee.

"This'll just take a sec," she says, turning to Eli.

He starts making these swishy noises, ticking his head back and forth while he cranks it all the way to one side. All of a sudden, he starts chugging again, making one long spray of spit as he rotates his head back.

I cover my head. "Knock it off!"

Sofía is bent over laughing when Eli stops and wipes his mouth. "I'm gonna go practice my laser sounds. See you!"

I swat at him as he barrels past us and out the end of the tube.

"You're so lucky you get to see his concert," Sofía says when he's gone, wiping spit from her forehead.

"You want me to ask Aunt Kathy if you can come?"

She brightens. "Really?"

"If you want."

Her face falls then. "That's okay." She sighs. "It sounds like a family thing."

I roll my eyes. "Well, you're not missing anything. Eli barely hangs out with me when Riley's home. He's too busy following his brother around."

"Don't you like him?" Sofía asks.

"Riley?" I shrug. "He's fine. He just doesn't pay attention to us." Before he left for college, he was always at swim practice or in his room in the basement. When he did come out, Eli would bounce around trying to get him to watch while he blew spit bubbles or ate paper or something. Then Riley would disappear into the basement again, and Eli would be quiet and sulky until I stopped trying to cheer him up and went home.

I'm not gonna lie: I didn't like being ignored. But the worst part was that I knew it hurt Eli's feelings, and I couldn't do anything to stop it.

But now that I'm a superhero, maybe I can help!

I pull the Rainbow Ring out of my shirt. Maybe

I can use Mind Control to distract Eli. Or to make Riley pay attention to him.

I wonder how it works—if it's like changing channels in my brain to control different people.

I have to find out before Riley gets home.

Sofía starts to climb out of the slide. "Four square?" she says.

"I thought we were practicing my brain powers!"

"But the bell's gonna ring."

"Just once more? Please?"

"Meena . . ." Sofía sits down again and starts working her jaw back and forth. She takes a deep breath and says quickly, "What if the Ring doesn't have powers?"

I chuckle. "Then it isn't much of a magic ring."

She gazes at me.

"Hang on." I stare at her. "You don't believe me?"

She twists the end of her braid. "I just think that . . . well, what difference does it make?"

I cross my arms. "Sofía María Rodríguez González." I use all her names so she knows I mean it. "That's like saying, 'What difference does it make if processed cheese food isn't really cheese, and Pop Rocks aren't made out of pop *or* rocks'? It makes all the difference in the world!"

She doesn't say anything, but I study the crinkle in her forehead and how she's twisting her hair into a tight little rope down the length of her shoulder.

She isn't trying to being mean, I realize. She just doesn't think there's anything special about me.

"Hey." She scootches over and bumps my shoulder with hers. "Even if you're not a superhero, you're still you. That's not so bad, right?"

That's not even enough for her to give me a one-and-only-best-friends bracelet. I can't look at her anymore. Instead, I look at the beads around my wrist. I used mostly purple, but it's the single yellow bead that stands out. Because it's the only one.

Sofía taps her foot against mine. "Right?" she says again.

"Yeah, I guess," I mutter.

The bell rings.

We climb out of the slide, pick up our backpacks, and make our way across the playground. I scuffle my feet through the wood chips, then the grass, then over the blacktop. I drag my feet so much that by the time we line up with the third grade, we have to stand all the way in the back.

"Go ahead, first graders," I hear the playground monitor say.

What if I'm not a superhero? Then I'm just my plain old regular self. Not one of a kind—just another kid. Like everyone else.

I kick my feet against the ground, staring at

my feet so long that at first I don't notice that the line of little kids isn't moving. "First graders," the monitor says again, "you can go on in."

"That's her," says a small voice.

I look up. The whole first grade is stuck behind their line leader: a little girl with curly black hair sproinging out of her pigtails.

The girl who walked in front of the van.

She's staring at me.

She tugs on the kid next to her. "That's the girl I told you about," she says, pointing right at me. She raises her voice, like she's making an announcement to the whole class. "She saved me. My mom said so."

Other little kids turn their heads. The playground monitor tries to wave them in, but they stay right there, standing on their toes to get a look at me over the line of second graders.

"I was there," Aiden says. "I saw it." All the kids are buzzing now. Heads turn toward me, staring.

I suck in my breath and take a step back.

Then I stand up straighter and hike my backpack higher. I tilt my chin up and set my jaw. When I clear my throat, I swear I hear a swell of music behind me.

I give the girl a nod. "Just doing my duty," I say.

This would be the perfect time to raise my fist in the air and lift myself up, up, and away.

But I don't know how to do that yet, so I salute instead.

Then I turn into the wind and gaze out at the horizon so the whole first grade can see me in profile, like the label on the side of the can when someone takes a drink in a soda commercial.

The lines start to move. Kids whisper and point all around me as I stride down the hall, holding my head high.

When we get to our cubbies, I turn and raise my eyebrows at Sofía. *Well?*

She bites her lip and shrugs. *Maybe.*

And I can't help it. I grin.

I *am* a superhero.

6

My head is buzzing as I put everything in my cubby and follow Sofía into the classroom. While papers shuffle onto desks and the pencil sharpener whizzes, I stare out the window, replaying the scene of how I saved that girl in my mind. I picture my leap from the curb and the way everybody turned to stare.

Only this time, I imagine myself in a cape.

A hand rests on my shoulder. I stiffen. Mrs. D is gazing down at me, a crinkle in her forehead. "Still with us?" she asks quietly.

I nod, feeling the back of my neck get hot. She's checking to see if I'm daydreaming or having one of my space-out seizures.

At least she didn't snap in my face this time.

"I asked if you're having school lunch today," she says.

"I brought mine."

Mrs. D makes a mark on the lunch slip and hands it to Maddy to take to the office.

I guess she's on Lunch Patrol this week. Lucky.

"Take out your writing journals, please," Mrs. D says. "The topic sentence is on the board."

I look around my pod of desks. On my right, Pedro is poking his pencil through a pink eraser. On my left, Eli is making *pew-pew* noises while he takes out his journal. Across from me, Sofía has already started writing.

I pick up my pencil. But instead of writing, I rest my chin in my hand and picture myself soaring through the sky, my cape flapping in the wind behind me.

The rest of the day is school as usual. Mrs. D doesn't hang my magic wand painting with the rest of the pandas because I didn't follow directions. She marks me down in spelling just because I like "fotograf" better than how everyone else writes it. She even corrects the way I print my own name just because I won't use that weird cursive Z that droops below the line.

But you know what? Who cares if I have to write and paint the same as everyone else? Even Superman has to blend in to keep his true identity a secret. I might have to be careful not to stand out too much in school.

That's okay. I know who I really am. Even better, Sofía does too.

So I don't make a big deal out of it, but all day I keep on the lookout for rescue missions. My skin feels tingly and alive, which must be exactly how spider-sense feels. Everywhere I look, it seems like someone needs my help, and I am right there, in the nick of time, every time.

BAM! I pick up a couple of empty milk cartons next to the trash.

ZAP! I share my blue marker with Nora when hers dries out.

POW! I hold the door for Mrs. D when she's carrying a stack of books. "Why, thank you, Meena," she says.

I nod. "Ma'am."

For once in my life, I even watch my clip go up instead of down on the behavior chart.

"That's very thoughtful of you, Meena." *CLIP!*

"What good sharing, Meena." *CLIP!*

"You've been such a good helper today, Meena." *CLIP!*

The last time Mrs. D snaps my clothespin into place, I can't believe my eyes. That's *my* clip at the top of the chart, right there next to At My Best!

"Is this your first time?" Mrs. D asks me, her eyes twinkling.

I nod, unable to speak.

"You know what that means," she says.

It means the Rainbow Ring *does* have special

powers. It has to. No way could I have done this on my own.

"What reward would you like to pick?" Mrs. D asks.

I blink at her. All around me, kids start to chatter.

"Extra recess," says Aiden.

"Bonus snack," says Eli.

"Prize drawer for everyone," says Nora.

Oh my gosh, that's right!

The first time someone clips to the top of the chart, they get to pick a reward for the *whole class*! It's supposed to help us root for each other, but I forgot all about it. Everyone else got their rewards ages ago, but I've never made it to the top before!

I sit up on my knees. "Can we play elimination?" I ask.

Mrs. D checks the clock and grabs her whistle from her desk. "I think we have time for that."

I pump my fists in the air. The class cheers. This Ring is the best thing ever!

Mrs. D lets me lead the way to the gym. I feel shiny and sparkly striding down the hall, the Ring bouncing on its shoestring against my chest. We used to play elimination at recess, but my class made so many kids in the other grades cry that now we're only allowed to play it by ourselves, and only on special occasions.

Like when one of us becomes a superhero!

Lin and Pedro almost always win. They run fast and throw hard, and they never drop the ball. But it's still fun to see who can stay in the game the longest. Now we gather in the center of the gym as Mrs. D grabs a playground ball. We get quiet as she steps into the middle of the circle. The whistle rattles on the chain around her neck. We stand still, waiting, heads down, bodies tense. The air smells like disinfectant and rubber mats.

Mrs. D puts the whistle to her lips. Then she throws the ball straight up in the air and steps back from the circle.

Tweeet!

We're off! Everyone breaks for the ball. Pedro gets it first and whips around. Kids shriek and sneakers squeak as we run the other way. He's only allowed three big steps before he throws. One, two, three . . . *SMACK!* The ball hits Nora in the leg. She goes to sit out while Maddy picks up the ball and chases Lin into the corner. Maddy throws, but Lin catches it in the air. Maddy is out!

Lin looks around then bounds forward, aims low, and thumps the boy next to me in the ankle as he scampers away. Out!

I scoop up the ball and hit a girl in the shoulder. Out! I dive for the ball again, step one-two-three, and whack someone else. Another kid down!

Eli picks up the ball, turns to me, and winds up. *Not me, not me, not me!* I always drop the ball! I hold my arms out, bracing myself for the stinging smack against my chest. But at the last second, Aiden runs past, and Eli throws at him instead. He misses, and Aiden scoops up the ball and whaps Eli! Then Pedro rebounds the ball and throws out Aiden.

One kid after another goes to the bench. In a few minutes, there are only three of us left—and I'm one of them! The Ring must be making me faster or harder to see.

The next time Pedro recovers the ball, Lin and I retreat to opposite corners. Just then, Mrs. D blows her whistle and calls, "Half-court!" Half the gym is out of bounds now. Lin and I edge closer, huddling in the corner farthest from Pedro. After his three big steps, he's still too far away to throw us out. For a few seconds, he just stands there dribbling, sizing us up.

Then he nods at Lin. She nods back.

Hang on. . . . They're ganging up on me!

I scowl and grab hold of my Rainbow Ring. *Not today, kids!*

One, two, three—Pedro closes the distance between us. He bounces the ball into the corner so Lin can grab it and throw me out.

I race forward, but Lin is blocking me! We

shove against each other, grunting. Just as Lin lunges for the ball, I hurtle myself on top of it.

The kids on the bleachers gasp. There's a split second when we both freeze. I'm flat on the floor, the ball trapped under my stomach, too surprised to move.

Then Lin turns to run.

I scramble up, chase one, two, three steps after her, and throw.

Her whole body flinches upright when the ball hits her in the back.

There's a great big whoop from across the gym. Lin turns to me, her eyes wide.

Holy hamster, I got her!

I'm so stunned, watching Lin shuffle off to the sidelines, that I forget to rebound the ball.

"Look out!" Sofía cries.

Too late. Pedro rushes over and grabs it. I back away, into the corner. He's right across from me, his eyes gleaming.

I hold my breath, square my shoulders, and wait.

One, two, three—Pedro throws at my legs. I jump—miss! The ball bounces off the wall. He grabs it, closes in, and throws at my shoulder. I leap to the side and hear it smack the wall—miss! He grabs it again. He's right in front of me!

I open my arms and close my eyes.

SMACK!

Silence.

Then cheering. "He's out! Pedro's out!"

I blink my eyes open. Slowly, everything comes into focus: Pedro staring at me, his mouth hanging open. The rest of the class is across the gym, jumping and shouting.

My chest is stinging. I look down.

The ball is in my arms.

I caught it. I actually caught it!

Everyone rushes over and crowds around, almost knocking me over. I look above their heads for Sofía, the only one left standing by the bleachers. She's shaking her head and smiling.

That's all I see before the throng of kids presses me out of the gym, like I'm in a parade, band playing, streamers flying. Even though I'm pretty sure my feet never leave the floor, if feels like they hoist me onto their shoulders and carry me down the hall.

7

All week long, I feel my powers growing.

I'm still not exactly sure what they are, but I'm definitely different all over. I feel strong. Electric, even. Everywhere I look, I see problems to solve and people to save.

Other kids must feel it too, because they pick me for their teams. They try to sit by me at lunch. One of the first graders even asks for my autograph! Everyone treats me like a hero.

Everyone except Sofía, that is. She doesn't treat me any differently at *all*.

When the other kids drag me away to play kickball, Sofía goes off to help Eli with his foghorn. When we pick partners for a social studies project, she pairs up with Lin instead of me—just because Lin asked her first. Then, when we stay in for recess, and I think it's finally going to be just the two of us, she invites Maddy and Nora to stay in too!

It's starting to get on my nerves.

At least we can test my powers some more

when we go to her house after school on Friday. It's been hard to figure out what I can do with everyone crowding around me this week. Maybe when we're alone, I'll perform a feat so amazing that Sofía will *have* to be impressed.

I'm bursting to get started, but we're barely two steps out of the building after school when a blur of rusty hair and sneakers goes flying past.

"Hey, Eli!" Sofía yells.

He turns around but keeps jogging in place on the sidewalk. "What?"

At least he's talking instead of blasting that police siren he's been working on.

"Are you ready for your concert?"

Eli grins. "I just have to practice my armpit farts. Riley gets home tonight!"

"Do you have plans?" Sofía asks.

"We'll probably hang out, just the two of us." Eli brightens. "I'm going to show him my new chickens and my walnut collection, and then we can stay up late and watch a scary movie and see who can eat the most jawbreakers. Maybe we'll even sleep out in the igloo!"

"When are the rest of us coming over?" I ask.

"I want to go with him in the morning to swim laps, so maybe after that. Hey! You want to hear me burp the alphabet?"

I grab Sofía's wrist to make a run for it, but

she plants her feet and pulls away. "Yeah," she says.

So I'm stuck there while Eli swallows a big gulp of air and starts croaking out letters.

"A-B-C . . ." He gasps. "D-E-F-G . . ."

By the time he gets to Z, he's red in the face and breathless, but Sofía bounces on her toes and starts clapping. "That was awesome," she squeals.

Eli smiles, the tips of his ears turning pink. "Riley can do it all in one breath," he says, "but I'll keep practicing. See you!" He turns and runs for home, holding up his hand to wave without looking back.

Sofía giggles as she watches him go. I cross my arms at her. "You act like that was the greatest thing ever," I say.

She smirks. "It *was* pretty great."

I lower my voice to a fierce whisper. "I can control people's minds. I might even be able to fly. What's so exciting about Eli's burps?"

She shrugs. "He worked really hard at them."

I shake my head. Whatever. I'll show her something a zillion times better.

Just as soon as I figure out what I can do.

Sofía lives on the first floor of a yellow house with white shutters a few blocks from school. Her dad works at night and sleeps during the day, so we creep up the porch steps, push through the front door, and set down our things as quietly as we can. When Sofía whisper-calls to the kitchen, her mom glides down the hall in a plushy lavender tracksuit. It looks so soft that I get a little jealous when she hugs Sofía—until she opens her arms to me, and I get a turn.

I always like listening to them talk to each other. Pretty much all the Spanish I know is my colors and numbers up to ten, so I never quite get over feeling impressed that Sofía knows two words for everything. Sometimes I quiz her, just to be sure. "Fruit," I say. "*Fruta*," she says. "Flowers," I say. "*Flores*." Sometimes the words sound so different that I think she might be trying to trick me. "Trash," I say. "*Basura*." See what I mean?

Sofía's cat threads his way through our legs, purring like a motorboat. His fur is spotted black and white and orange, so she named him Oriol—after the bird. "*Hola, cariño*," she says, stroking his tail.

Even Oriol knows more Spanish than I do.

Sofía's mom says something else and heads to the kitchen.

"She said to play outside," Sofía says. "She'll bring us a snack."

My favorite thing to eat at Sofía's house is this soft candy that you scoop out of its own little tray with a stick. It comes in a bunch of flavors, but the best one is like a teeny little box of Neapolitan ice cream, except it's not cold, and you get to eat the whole thing yourself.

I decide to test out my powers right then and there.

While I follow Sofía out the back door, I half close my eyes and fill my mind with the name of the candy, pushing it toward Sofía's mom like I'm making a big wave in the bathtub. WHOOSH—*Duvalín*. WHOOSH—*Duvalín Tri Sabor*.

Right when we plop down on the back stoop, Sofía's mom appears in the doorway, waving two packets of Duvalín.

BAM!

When she's gone, I give Sofía a smug look. "I told her to bring these with my mind."

Sofía stops peeling back the plastic wrapper. "You're testing your powers on my mom?"

"Sure."

Her face reddens. "You shouldn't do that without asking, Meena."

"Why not? She didn't even know."

"Have you been trying to mind-control *me*?"

"No!"

"You'd better not."

"Geez." I stab my candy. "What's the big deal?"

"It just seems like stealing." Sofía scrapes strawberry goo onto her plastic stick. "Besides, if

you do have powers, you should use them to help
people, not just to get stuff you want."

"What do you mean, 'if'?"

Sofía sucks on her stick and doesn't answer.

She *still* isn't sure? Well, how am I supposed to
prove it to her? It's been a whole week, and I haven't
seen a single person run out of a burning building
or dangle from a cliff.

Behind us, the cat flap in the door slaps shut as
Oriol slinks through. He stops, points his tail, and
starts *ack-ack*-ing at a sparrow that's grooming
itself at the top of Sofía's old kiddie slide.

She clicks her teeth at him. *"Calmate, tonto."*

"How about Oriol?" I ask. "Can I test my powers on him?"

She narrows her eyes at me. "What do you
want to make him do?"

"Nothing bad. I'll just call him with my mind."

She laughs. "He's a cat. He won't come."

I let out a huffy breath. "I don't get it," I say. "One
minute, you don't want me to use my powers, and the
next minute, you act like they don't work anyway."

She presses her lips together. "Fine. Go ahead."

I set down my candy and step closer to Oriol.
I crouch down and hold out my hand. *Here, kitty
kitty*, I think.

Oriol stops *ack*-ing and looks at me, his yellow
eyes round and glassy.

Come here, Oriol.

He reaches a paw in front of him. Then the other.

That's it, come to Meena.

He stretches his hindquarters into the air.

You can do it, Oriol. Good kitty!

Then he rolls onto his back and shows his tummy to the sky.

Sofía covers her mouth, her eyes flickering with laughter.

"Whatever," I say, blushing. "I bet it would work if I knew his language."

"What, cat?"

"No, Spanish."

Suddenly, Oriol flips onto his feet and zips up

the little slide, chasing the sparrow away.

Hang on . . . That gives me an idea.

Maybe I can leap tall buildings in a single bound!

I shoo Oriol off the slide and drag it to the middle of the yard so I can use it as a ramp. Then I close my eyes, take a deep breath, and picture myself soaring high over the roof, as graceful as a ballerina.

Except in a cape.

"Watch this," I say, jogging back a ways. I put my head down, stamp my feet like a bull, and take off running, pumping my arms and stomping my feet against the ground.

Only just as I'm about to run up the slide and ramp into the air, Oriol screeches.

I stop short.

Sofía springs to her feet. "Oriol."

He hunches down and hisses at me, his ears flat, tail smacking.

I back away. "What's his problem?"

"You scared him." She takes a step forward and reaches out to him. "*Estás bien, gatito,*" she says in a low voice.

He glares at me, then turns and nuzzles her hand.

I shoot Oriol a look. "Can we just put him inside for a while?"

"I haven't seen him all day," Sofía says, stroking the top of his head.

My heart sinks. I haven't been over in weeks, but she doesn't seem to care about that.

"What are you trying to do, anyway?" she asks.

"Forget it," I mutter.

I'll just figure this out on my own. I'll practice at home until I know for sure what my powers are. Then, when the time is right, and she least expects it, I'll be ready.

BAM!

It doesn't matter what we do now, so I let Sofía pick. We waste the rest of the afternoon watching a bunch of those bird videos she likes. I wish I could mind-control *myself*, but all the powers in the world couldn't make me like bird stuff. I sit there, staring at the screen and sucking on my plastic stick long after the candy is gone.

And just once, even though I know I shouldn't, I *WHOOSH* a thought at her as hard as I can.

Believe me.

8

It's pouring rain when I wake up on Saturday, which foils my plan to test out my flying on the school playground while nobody is there.

When I come downstairs, Mom is already at the computer in her bathrobe. She takes off her glasses, rubs her eyes, and motions me over. "Want to guess how long I've been up?" she asks, wrapping me in a hug.

"An hour."

"Two, actually."

"Why?"

"Tax season."

There's a chart on her screen—rows of gray rectangles, filled with tiny black numbers. "How can you spend two hours looking at that?"

She gives me a twinkly look. "I don't mind. I like getting everything in order. It's beautiful in its own way."

"It'd be nice if it were beautiful in an *actual*

way." I get out the Rainbow Pops cereal and pour the last of it into a bowl.

"I think we're out of milk," Mom says.

"That's okay." I count up the colors in my bowl—no purple. Which reminds me . . . "Hey, when are we painting my room?"

"Depends how much I get done this week." She stands up. "You need anything before I go shower?"

"Something purple."

"Grapes in the fridge," she says. She kisses me on top of the head and scuffs away in her slippers.

I grab a few grapes and sit crunching on dry cereal, listening to the patter of rain and the soft whir of Mom's computer. I try to hum a matching pitch to make it sound more like music, but I can't keep my eyes off the dull gray rows. They're the same color as my bedroom. I'm just about to turn the screen away when I feel the twitch of an Inspiration.

My crunching slows down. I scan over all those numbers, trapped inside their little gray cells.

I know what that's like.

I can save them, I realize. So what if they're only numbers? I can save Mom, too. She shouldn't have to stare at that boring, black and gray screen hour after hour.

I scoot up to the computer and get started.

When I click on the drop-down menu, a grid of colors appears on the screen like a miniature paint chip display. There are so many to choose from! For a long time, I click and highlight and change colors. I pick a new font, too—something cheerful this time. I don't know how long I'm at it, but pretty soon, the whole screen looks like a rainbow. I'm just about to save my work when I hear a gasp.

Mom is standing in the doorway in jeans and a sweater, her hair wet around her shoulders. "What are you doing?"

I jump up and throw out my arms. "Surprise!"

She hurries over and stares at the screen. "Did you change my numbers to *Comic Sans*?"

"No need to thank me," I say. "I was just doing my—"

"No, no, no . . ." She claps her hands over her cheeks and sinks into the chair. "I have to get it back."

I blink. "Why?"

"Seriously, Meena." She starts to click frantically. "I can't submit it like this. *How do I get it back?*"

"There's an undo button. It's right—"

"Don't touch it!"

I take a step away.

She starts clicking undo over and over, draining all the color from the screen. I feel it leaking out of me, too. "I thought you'd like it," I mutter.

"What I'd like," she says, "is for you to leave my work alone."

I shake my head and stomp my bowl over to the sink. She's like someone on a crumbling ledge that won't jump into Superman's arms. Some people don't know what's good for them.

I head upstairs and plop onto the floor of my workshop. This is probably a bad time to ask if there are any railroad tracks around here, in case somebody's getting tied up. Or if there are any earthquakes scheduled, in case people start falling into the cracks.

I guess I could work on my supersuit some more. I should have grabbed a milk jug, but no way am I sneaking past Mom to the recycling bin now.

Maybe if I made my body flat enough, I could slide through the doors, stretch around corners, and slip past her!

I try wedging my head under the door, but it doesn't fit. My fingers go through, no problem, but the meaty part of my hand gets stuck. I let out all my breath and suck in my stomach, but I still can't get through. I sigh, pick up Raymond, and kiss his hooves. "Worth a try," I tell him.

Maybe I can float the milk jug up here with my mind!

I press my hand against the door and grab hold of the Rainbow Ring, imagining the recycling bin by the back door. I picture a milk jug floating silently past Mom, close to the floor, where she won't spot it. I concentrate on reeling it in, up the stairs, down the hall to my—

KNOCK, KNOCK, KNOCK!

I lurch away from the door, my heart pounding.

But when I creak it open and peek out, it's just Rosie, holding Pink Pony by the tail. "What are you doing?" she asks. When she scratches the front of her neck, the pink beads on her bracelet click.

"Working," I say. "Go away."

"Can I help?"

I'm about to tell her no when I realize something. Maybe instead of moving the milk jug with my mind, I accidentally commanded Rosie here to *get it for me.*

That's almost as good!

"Actually," I say lowering my voice, "I do need something."

She leans in closer. "What?" she loud-whispers.

"A milk jug. From the recycling."

She nods, very serious, then darts down the stairs. I make sure to channel my mind control so Mom doesn't get suspicious. *You don't see her—* WHOOSH. *You aren't interested in what she's doing at all.*

Then Rosie is back, handing the jug through the door.

"Did Mom ask what you were doing?"

"Nope. She was working." *Yes!* Rosie pokes her head in. "What are you making?"

I squint at her. "If I tell you, you can't tell anyone else. Promise?"

"Not even Mom?"

I start to close the door.

"Wait," she says quickly. "I promise."

I wave her in and shut the door. "It's a suit."

Her eyes get wide. "What kind of suit?"

"A supersuit."

"What for?"

I think fast. "Let's just say I met a superhero."

"What? Lucky!"

"And let's just say this superhero asked me to make them a suit."

Rosie sighs. "You're good at making stuff."

"Right? So how would you like to bring me some supplies?"

She perks back up. "What do you need?"

I get *lots* of good work out of Rosie. She fetches a plastic tablecloth from the picnic supplies, a snorkeling mask from the swim bag, and a garbage bag from under the kitchen sink. When I get thirsty, she fills my water bottle and brings it up. She even grabs Mom's galoshes and stuffs the toes with crumpled paper so they don't fall off my feet.

"I need a utility belt," I tell Rosie next. "How

do you think Mom would feel about lending me some tools?"

It's hard to tell through the swim mask that's strapped over the eyeholes I cut in the jug, but Rosie looks doubtful. "Not good," she says.

"Okay." My voice sounds flat and muffled in here, and my breath is making it wet. "Then just grab the pinchy thing, the wheely-deely thing, and the sunction thing. And you'd better leave the hammer." I'll just have to kick down doors with my feet.

When Rosie creeps downstairs, I check out my suit in the mirror. As long as I keep the mask on, you can't tell it's me in here!

I clomp back and forth across the room. The galoshes make a floppy, rubbery sound when I run. I'm so busy trying to get the picnic cape to flutter behind me that I forget to protect Rosie.

"Meena Zee, come down here!"

Mom.

I throw off my costume and hurry to the kitchen. The tools are on the table, and Mom is sitting with her arms crossed. Rosie is slumped in a chair, not looking at me.

"Give us a minute, please, Rosie," Mom says.

Rosie gives me *I'm sorry* eyes and slinks away.

Mom rests her elbows on the table. "What are you up to?"

"Nothing."

"Then why have you had your sister running around all morning?"

"We're working on a project."

She leans forward. "*Who's* working on it?"

I toe the floor. "I am. But Rosie's helping me," I add quickly.

Mom gazes at me for a long time. "You know, one of these days, Rosie is going to wake up and realize that you're taking advantage of her."

"You said to include her," I say, the back of my neck getting hot.

"That's not what I meant, and you know it."

"But she likes it!"

"Rosie doesn't want to be your errand girl, Meena," Mom says. "She wants to be your equal."

"We're *not* equal. I'm older than her."

(Plus, I'm a superhero.)

Mom sighs and rubs her forehead. "Stop ordering her around," she says. "It's not good for her. It's not good for you to get your way all the time either. But for now" — she nods toward the sink — "the least you can do is wash the breakfast dishes."

"What? It's Rosie's turn!"

"I think she's done enough for you today."

I huff over to the sink. It isn't fair! No one ever made Superman wash the dishes! You'd better believe he never had to do his sister's chores, either. You know why?

Because he didn't have one! Lucky.

I put in the plug and turn the water onto full blast, my stomach clenching in a tight little ball. When I squeeze in the soap, a cloud of lemon-fresh steam rises all around me. I breathe it in a few times, my stomach relaxing a little. Okay, so I don't really mind having a sister. Not usually. But what good are my powers if I can't use them for myself once in a while?

Then I remember what Sofía said. About using my powers for good.

I turn off the faucet and look at the cups and bowls peeking up through the bubbles. I'm supposed to fight crime. Defeat villains. Defend the public. I'm supposed to help people. That's what I started out doing.

Why do I keep getting sidetracked?

I pick up a bowl and rub the sponge over it then rinse off the suds and set it on the rack. I wash the next dish, and the next, concentrating on each one, lining them up in a neat little row to dry, clean as a whistle. For a while, there's no sound in the kitchen but the water trickling and Mom clicking and the rain tapping against the windows.

Then the back door rattles, and Dad steps in, soaking wet in his running tights. "Hey, champ," he says when he sees me.

"You ran in the rain?" I ask.

"You bet. It's invigorating! See?" He comes over, shakes his head like a dog, and splatters me.

"Dad!"

He snickers and ruffles my hair then picks up a dish towel and starts drying the back of his head. "I ran by your sister's," he says to Mom. "She said Riley didn't come home last night."

Mom looks up from her computer. "What? Is he okay?"

"He's fine. He went on a road trip with some friends at the last minute instead. He was already halfway to Florida when he called."

I pull the plug out of the sink. "He's not coming at all?"

"He said he'd come next weekend," Dad says, "at the end of his break."

"But Eli wanted to do a concert for him," I say, drying my hands on my shirt.

"I guess he'll have to do it next week."

But that wasn't all he had planned. I think of Eli running home from school yesterday, and my chest starts to hurt. I imagine him waiting in his living room last night with a big bag of jawbreakers. I picture him sitting alone in his room right now. I swallow hard. "He wanted Riley to take him to the pool this morning," I say.

Mom sighs. "He can't exactly do that from Florida."

I put my hand over the Rainbow Ring. "But I can."

Mom tilts her heads at me. "You think he'll still want to go?"

"Of course he will. He loves it there."

Dad looks at Mom and shrugs. "It can't hurt to offer."

I make a move for Mom's phone. "I'll call him. Can you drop us off?"

"Honey . . ." She grabs the phone away. "We can't just leave you there."

I stare at her. "Why not? We go swimming by ourselves all the time."

"You did last summer, but things are different now. If you had a seizure in the water . . ." Her voice trails off.

I wave my hand in the air. I'm sure the Rainbow Ring would keep me safe, but all I can say out loud is, "That's what lifeguards are for."

"Lifeguards scan the area," Mom says. "Someone needs to watch *you*. Besides that, Rosie will want to go, and she hasn't passed the swim test yet." She smacks her hands on her thighs and starts packing up her computer. "We'll all go."

"But you're working!"

"I can work anywhere."

I roll my eyes. I don't care who else is coming. This is my chance to help Eli and to use my powers for good—to be the kind of hero Sofía can believe in.

It's Meena to the rescue!

9

Aunt Kathy looks tired when she answers the door, her red curls wild around her face. "Eli," she calls.

Rain patters all around, but the tiny roof over their stoop keeps me dry. Down the hall, Eli shuffles out of his room, his shoulders slumped.

"At least you still get to swim, right?" she says, holding out his bag.

"But what if he changes his mind?" Eli whines. "What if he's on his way now?"

Aunt Kathy hangs the bag across his body. "If he shows up, I'll send him over." She strokes his hair. "But I don't think that's likely."

Eli scowls and pulls away from her. He grabs the strap of his bag and pushes past me.

Aunt Kathy sighs, her eyes following him down the front walk as the rain pelts his head and shoulders. "Thanks for trying," she says.

"Don't worry." I give her arm a pat. "I've got this."

Rosie scootches to the middle seat to make room for us, her arm floaties squeaking.

"Hey, buddy," Dad says from the front.

"Wanna see my bracelet?" Rosie asks, sticking her wrist in Eli's face.

Eli doesn't say anything— just clicks in his seat belt, leans his head against the window, and stares out into the rain.

The indoor pool is the noisiest place on earth.

The hot tub groans and bubbles. Water crashes onto the splash pad floor. Kids shriek, whistles tweet, and lifeguard voices boom through megaphones: "Walk! Walk!"

Mom spreads a towel on a lounge chair while Dad and Rosie go to play in the shallow end. I whip off my hoodie while Eli steps out of one sandal, then the other.

"Wanna go off the diving boards?" I ask, shouting over the crashing and splashing.

He shrugs.

"The lifeguard there only has to watch two or three kids at a time," Mom says, "so I'll do some work. But if you go anywhere else, come and tell me." She squints at my neck. "What's that?"

The Rainbow Ring! I clap my hand over it. "It's a good-luck charm," I stutter, thinking fast.

She holds out her hand. "Give it to me."

I take a step back. "Why?"

"I don't want you swimming with something tied around your neck."

I clutch the Ring harder.

"It's not safe, Meena. I'll hold it for you."

I hesitate. Warm, bleachy air prickles my nose. Slowly, I pull the Ring over my head and watch Mom stuff it in her pocket. My chest feels empty without it.

I give myself a shake. I can still do this. I swallow and stand up straighter. Operation Cheer Up Eli is underway!

"Come on," I say and lead the way around the pool to the low diving board. "You want to go first?"

Eli shakes his head, staring into space.

I climb onto the board and take off running. "Octopus Jump!" I throw myself off the end, arms flailing. Cold shocks my body, and water muffles my ears, then right away I feel warm all over. I kick to the top and swim for the side, blinking hard.

"Do a cannonball," I yell to Eli.

He shuffles to the end of the board and stands there, looking across the water. I follow his eyes, but there's nothing over there except the entrance.

"Let's go, buddy," the lifeguard calls from her chair.

Eli steps off, barely making a splash.

I groan. "That was boring," I shout when he surfaces. "Come on. Let's try it again."

We go off the board a few more times. I do a cannonball, a twist, and a flip that turns into a belly flop. When it's Eli's turn, I *WHOOSH* cheerful thoughts his way. *I love the pool! I'm so glad I came!*

But each time, he walks to the end of the board, looks across the water, and steps off.

Maybe we should have started with the most fun thing in this place. "Want to go down the big slide?" I ask.

His shoulder twitches a shrug.

I look over at Mom. She's focused on the computer in her lap. "Let's go," I say.

We climb the winding staircase. I grip the railing. Water drips on us through the grated steps above. While Eli waits his turn at the top, I concentrate on filling him up with happiness. I imagine pouring it into him with a pitcher until he's brimming over with one thrilling thought: *I'm having the time of my life!* Finally, when the lifeguard gives the okay, Eli sits in the rushing water at the top of the slide, gives a tiny push, and lets the current pull him down, slow as sludge.

You've got to be kidding me.

I plop down next. When the lifeguard nods, I put my head down and push off hard, paddling against the walls, leaning forward, making myself go faster and faster until I ride up the sides and almost flip over.

SPLASH!

The slide dumps me out at the bottom.

I break the surface again and smear water out of my eyes. "*That's* how it's done," I say to the pair of feet by the ladder.

But they're not Eli's. They're Mom's.

"You were supposed to tell me if you left the diving area," she says.

I look up at her. "Yeah, but there's, like, one lifeguard per person over here."

"Just tell me if you go anywhere else."

"Why?"

"Because I want to know where to look for you. Got it?"

I climb out, squeeze water out the ends of my hair, and grunt.

She gives me a hard look and heads back to her chair.

I turn to Eli. "Want to go again? It's faster if you lean forward."

He doesn't look at me. "I'm getting in the hot tub."

"What? No! I can hardly breathe in that thing, and it makes me shrively."

"Then don't come." He heads to the bubbling

pool of grown-ups, slips in, and wades to the other side.

I stare at him. What the heck? He should be cheered up! Is this because Mom took the Ring? But I've been wearing it for a *week*! Some of its power should have rubbed off on me by now.

No. I thrust my shoulders back. I am saving that boy, whether he likes it or not.

I glance at Mom, settling into her chair again, then follow Eli.

I plop down at the edge of the hot tub and dip my toes in the piping hot water. He stares over my shoulder and flicks his cheek with his finger to make a dripping water sound.

And another.

And another.

"Meena!"

Not again.

Mom is standing over me, hands on her hips. "I *just* said—"

"You were working," I say. "I didn't want to bother you."

She rubs her forehead. "I will set it aside if I need to watch you. Now, are you going to do what I asked or not?"

"It'd be easier to remember if I had my good-luck charm."

Mom's lips pull into a line. "You're not having trouble remembering. You're having trouble obeying. Last chance." She strides back to her chair, flip-flops slapping.

I turn back to Eli, sitting in the steam, rusty hair plastered to his forehead. "Let's get kickboards and have a race."

He doesn't answer.

"Let's see how long we can hold our breath underwater."

He shakes his head.

"Let's play tag until the lifeguard yells at us."

"Not right now," he says.

My stomach starts to bubble like the water. I clench my fists and *WHOOSH* a tidal wave of happy thoughts toward him: *This is the best day ever!*

Eli's eyes light up.

It's working!

He stands up, looking over my shoulder, water streaming down his arms.

I turn and see a redheaded man coming through the entrance. A little girl hands him a towel. When I turn back, Eli's face falls. He sinks back into the hot tub.

"Are you waiting for Riley?" I ask. "Is that why you're sitting here? So you can watch the door?"

His eyes flick over to me, then away. "None of your business."

The heat in my stomach steams up through my chest and out my ears. "You aren't even trying to have fun."

He clenches his jaw.

"He's not coming, Eli. Everyone knows it!"

He covers his ears. "Shut up, Meena."

The grown-ups stop talking and stare at us.

"I'm trying to help," I say.

"Leave me alone!" Eli hangs his head and sinks even lower, the water is up to his chin. "Just leave me alone," he says again, his voice a whimper.

I don't get it. Riley ignores him. He lets Eli down.

And I'm right here! I could help him if he'd let me. I want to reach out and pull him to safety.

But he'd rather stay in the lake of fire.

I yank my feet out of the water. When I glance at Mom, she's standing at the edge of the kiddie area, clapping while Rosie does a back float.

I don't need her watching *me* like a little kid. I stomp over to the high diving board and start climbing.

Halfway up the ladder, my arms start to shake. My feet feel slippery, but I keep going. At the top, I clutch the railing, my heart beating hard. I grit my teeth and tiptoe out, forcing myself to where the railing ends and the board stretches over the water below.

I take deep breaths, swaying a little, looking around for people to save. A toddler teeters along the edge, but then his mom hurries over and takes his hand. A girl is about to dive into the shallow end, but a lifeguard stops her in time. Two kids duck underwater in the deep end, but right when I think they must be drowning, they bob back up.

The lifeguard tweets his whistle for me to go.

I jump off and plummet toward the water. I might not have a cape, but I swear that for a second I hang in midair before the blue surface hurtles toward me.

SMACK! The water closes around me. I paddle for a long time before I break through then take a big breath and swim under the ropes into the lap pool. I push off the wall, my body skimming under the water like an arrow, strong and powerful and free—like I'm flying.

My feet kick like thunder. I move my arms through the water, imagining that I'm clearing away evil, wiping out crime. The hair bands and pennies at the bottom of the pool look like cities to protect far below. I pretend to shoot lightning out my fingers and strike down villains. When my chest is throbbing, and I can't hold my breath any longer, I kick to the surface.

Mom is looking around, whipping her head one way, then another. She waves frantically to a lifeguard, then turns this way.

I take a gulp of air and duck underwater.

Maybe she didn't see me. I try to keep still, but my body floats up until my back sticks out of the water. Maybe I can sneak out and pretend I went to the bathroom. I kick myself to the wall, grab hold of the edge, and wipe the water from my eyes.

Mom's flip-flops are right in front of me.

She's glowering down, nostrils flaring, like she's about to start breathing fire. "Get out," she says. Her voice is quiet. Scary quiet. Eye-of-the-hurricane quiet.

"Um . . ." I push my hair back out of my eyes. "I forgot?"

"No, you didn't."

"I was only in the water for a minute," I say quickly.

Mom crouches down and leans her elbows on her knees. "How long do you think it would take a lifeguard to notice you having a seizure? How long do you think it takes to drown?"

I feel a rush of heat through my whole body. The concrete scrapes against my knee as I climb out. My skin prickles in the cool air.

Eli comes over, looking pale and wilty. "What's up, buddy?" Mom asks, her voice instantly kind.

"Would it be all right if I went home? I don't feel very good."

"Of course," she says gently, putting a hand on his head. "Meena's leaving too."

"What?" I say. "Why?"

Mom shoots me a look of pure fury. Her body seems to expand to fill the whole room. "Because you aren't listening. Because I asked you to follow one rule for your own safety, and you didn't."

I shrink away, my insides withering. I slink over to the lounge chair and pull on my clothes, my hair dripping onto my shirt, my suit soaking through everything.

Eli doesn't look at me.

Not that I'm looking at him.

Mom strides over to the shallow end, says something to Dad, then comes and grabs her things. She reaches into her pocket, blinks, and pulls out my Rainbow Ring, staring at it like she's never seen it before.

I reach to take it back. "At least can I have my—"

Mom holds up her hand like a crossing guard. "If I were you," she says, "I'd think really hard about whether this is the right time to ask me for anything."

She stuffs the Ring back into her pocket and storms toward the door.

10

I'm grounded for the rest of the weekend.

I don't get my Ring back either, because just when I think it's safe to ask for it on Sunday, Mom finds all the unfinished suckers I was saving at the back of my sock drawer and makes me wipe out the whole dresser!

The only thing I can do is start working on my superhero movie poster. I start with a circle in the middle of the paper and take my time drawing a rainbow burst spreading out around it, just like the Ring. In the center of the circle, I draw the outline of a person, but I leave it blank for now, since I'm still working on my suit. When I go to bed on Sunday, my mind is swirling with color.

But that night, I have the same dream over and over. I'm falling off the high dive. The pool below is empty, and I flail in the air, screaming, then jerk awake at the last second, right before I hit the cement.

Without the Ring, I can't even fly in my *dreams*.

On Monday morning, I'm so tired that I fall back asleep after Dad wakes me, and the next thing I know, Mom is shaking me. Dad has already left with Rosie, and I have to pull on my clothes and run out the door. I don't even have time to pack a lunch.

I'm halfway to school before I realize I *still* don't have my Ring.

I don't feel super without it. All morning, I'm groggy and mixed up. I think I even space out during our read-aloud book, because one minute Wilbur is going to try spinning a web like Charlotte, and then somehow I have a funny taste in my mouth, and I've missed the whole thing!

After that, I don't even feel like saving anybody. When Lin drops her pencil in the aisle, I watch it roll toward my foot and leave it there. When Mrs. D asks for a volunteer to pick up homework sheets while Nora is out sick, I keep quiet. When Pedro sneezes, I don't even say *Bless you.*

Eli still isn't looking at me.

Not that I'm looking at him.

By the time I shuffle down the hall to lunch, my stomach is starting to hurt too. Across the table, Sofía pops open her little can of apple juice, yanks the tab off the top, and hands it to me. I slip it into my pocket then wince at my tray and push it aside.

"You okay?" Sofía asks. She takes out her

neat and orderly lunch: cheese cubes, raisins, and an applesauce pouch that squirts straight into your mouth. They all sound terrible right now.

"I haven't had anything colorful to eat today," I mutter.

Just looking at the gray puddle of Salisbury steak makes my stomach do a somersault. If I had my Ring, maybe I could blink my eyes and make it disappear.

I close my eyes and rest my face on the table. It feels cool against my cheek, but the dirt-like smell of gravy makes my stomach clench like a fist.

"You want some candy?" Sofía asks.

That might help. I open my hand and feel the little round candies click together against my palm. I know without looking that she gave me one of each color.

"You want to stay in for recess today?" Sofía asks. "I need Mrs. D to help me with math."

"Okay," I say. "My stomach's kind of icky anyway." I pop a candy into my mouth, but right when I taste the sour burst of green apple, a wave of nausea washes over me. I sit up straight and suck in some air. My head is starting to spin now too.

"Yeah, you don't look so good," Sofía says.

I squeeze my eyes shut, but the seesaw feeling doesn't go away. All around me, kids chatter and laugh, but the sound seems to bend in the air, like music playing in a passing car.

I hold my head in my hands. I am *not* going to throw up.

"Meena?" Sofía's voice seems like it's coming from far away. But I can't answer her, because I'm sinking down onto the bench beneath me, curling up, clutching my stomach.

"Mr. Powell!" Sofía is shouting now, but her voice just keeps getting quieter as it fades farther into the distance.

My head hurts.

That's the first thing I notice. The smell of gravy is the second, then the metallic taste in my mouth.

I blink my eyes open. A fluorescent light panel. Someone's face.

"Hey, hon."

Mom? I try to sit up, but the sick feeling floods my stomach, and my head feels like a car that's being flattened by a monster truck.

"Stay still for me, okay?" She takes me in her arms and eases me back down.

I'm lying on something hard. The floor, I think. Turning my head, I see a green bean nearby, and the underside of a long table. "Where am I?" I say in a creaky voice.

"The lunchroom," Mom says.

Her face is coming into focus now. The hairs springing out of her ponytail make a frizzy halo around her head. She's sitting cross-legged on the floor next to me. I hear the dull clanging of spoons on metal.

"Where is everyone?" I ask.

"At recess."

Then why am I on the lunchroom floor? With my mom? And a headache?

Hang on.

"Did I have a seizure?" I ask.

She reaches over to stroke my hair. "Mm-hmm."

I groan. "How long?"

"It only lasted a minute, but you've been out for a while. I'll take you home when you're ready."

"Don't I have to go to the hospital?"

"No. The doctor said if it happened again we should just keep a close watch on you."

I close my eyes. This can't be happening. What kind of a superhero has seizures?

My eyes snap open. One without her Rainbow Ring. That's what kind.

I reach up and grope the empty spot by my neck. More clanging sounds come from the kitchen, along with the fake pine smell of cleaning spray. "Did Sofía call for someone?" I sort of remember. Almost.

"Yep. Mr. Powell had everybody go finish lunch in their classrooms."

That must have been exciting. I'm actually sorry I missed it. "Too bad they had to finish their steak," I say.

Mom chuckles softly. "Let's see if we can get you up." She helps me stand. A blanket that I didn't know was covering me falls to my feet. Mom picks it up and wraps it around my shoulders. "Okay so far?" she asks, putting her arm around me.

I nod. My legs aren't very strong, but I can walk.

"We'll take it slow."

We shuffle across the lunchroom and down the hall, my body heavy, my head throbbing. Rosie is in the main office, playing Go Fish with the secretary. When she sees us, she runs around the big desk and tries to hug me, but Mom steps in front of her. "Give her a few minutes, okay, sweetie?"

Rosie takes a step back and looks at me with big eyes. I try to give her a little smile, but it comes out a grimace instead. As Mom steers me out of the building, the bell rings, and the sound seems to pierce through my forehead.

As soon as we get home, I slump onto the couch. Mom tucks a blanket around me. Rosie runs upstairs and brings me Raymond, then leans in the doorway, sucking her fingers and looking at

me the same way she looked at her baby doll when its arm popped off—like I'm broken.

I curl away from her, my stomach starting to bubble hot, right through the ick. This shouldn't have happened. It *wouldn't* have if I'd had my Ring. I'm as strong and as healthy as anybody—even stronger!

Mom sits down at the other end of the couch and pulls my feet onto her lap. "Get some rest, okay? I'll be right here."

To spy on me.

My eyes are so heavy that I can't hold them open anymore, but I manage to whisper, "I need my Ring."

Mom is quiet for a few seconds. "Your what?" she asks finally.

"My Ring. From the pool."

"You mean your good-luck charm?"

I want to scream, *It's not a good-luck charm! It activates my powers! It makes me strong and special!* But even the silent screaming makes my head hurt, so instead I just mumble, "I need it."

My legs shift as she gets up. I hear a drawer in the kitchen open and close. When I look again, she's dangling the Ring over me. It spins and glints in the light. I try to reach for it, but my arm is too heavy.

"Here," Mom says, sliding it over my head.

I lift the Ring and stare at it, then through it—through the empty circle in the middle.

"Better?" Mom asks.

I nod and close my eyes, pressing the Ring to my chest. I'll be okay now. Everything will be okay.

It has to be.

It doesn't take long for the Ring to start working again. By the time I wake up that afternoon, I feel better—right back to my super self!

Too bad nobody treats me that way.

Rosie won't stop watching me from across the room. Dad ruffles my hair more than usual when he comes home. Mom sends me to bed at the regular time, even though I already had a *nap*!

Then, at breakfast Tuesday morning, Mom turns to Rosie and says, "Pop quiz. What would you do if Meena had a seizure on the way to school?"

Rosie sets down her milk and answers so fast that I know they've been practicing. "Turn her on her side, and call for help."

"Hang on," I say. "Rosie doesn't need to look out for me. I'm the big sister here!"

(And the only one with superpowers.)

"You look out for each other," Mom says.

"Mom?" Rosie asks, twisting her napkin.

"What if Meena has a seizure when we're crossing the street? What do I do?"

Mom looks uncomfortable. "That isn't very likely."

"But she might get run over."

"That's an excellent point," Dad says. He looks at me, rubs his chin, and then raises an eyebrow at Rosie. "Think you can drag your sister to the curb?"

Rosie gasps. I groan.

"I say grab her by the wrists," Dad continues. "Or no. The ankles might be easier. Let's practice." He claps his hands and stands up. "Meena. Lie down on the floor."

Rosie is giggling now.

"Dad," I say.

"Maybe we should practice in the driveway. The tile is too slippery."

"I'm fine."

"You want to try rolling her?"

"Dad!" I insist. "I am *completely fine*."

His eyes twinkle. He turns to Mom and shrugs. "She's fine. Let them go."

Rosie hops down, puts on her jacket and backpack, and turns to me. "Ready?" she asks. She doesn't wait for an answer before she leads the way outside.

"Wait up," I call, scrambling for my things.

As soon as I'm out the door, Rosie runs down

the block to the first crossing. By the time I catch up, she's already checking both ways for cars. She turns and holds out her hand, like *she's* the one helping *me* across.

I grab Rosie's wrist and step out in front of her, taking such big steps that I'm kind of dragging her.

If anyone around here is doing any helping, it's me.

But when we turn the corner, I see something that makes me forget all about who's in charge. A mattress is leaning against a tree by the curb. A rickety grill is sitting next to it, along with a wooden chair without any seat.

It's bulk trash day! This is the only day all month that people can put out trash that's too big for the bins.

I could furnish a whole *house* full of workshops with this stuff! I let go of Rosie and start running from pile to pile. Just look at this! There's a saggy couch with torn cushions, a lopsided lamp, and an empty spool for a garden hose. There's a lawn mower without an engine and a plastic cooler without a lid. There's even a TV as big as a dresser. I bet if you busted out the screen, you could climb inside and act out your own shows!

I'm so excited running around the heaps that I almost go right past the best thing of all.

Behind a stepladder that's missing some rungs,

I spot an office chair. It's red with stuffing coming out of the arms and a big splash of purple paint dried across the seat. But the wheels still wheel, and the seat still seats, and when I sit down and kick, it even spins around in a circle!

I drag it onto the sidewalk. "Wait here," I say to Rosie. "I need to run this home."

"We're supposed to go straight to school," she says.

"It'll only take a couple of minutes."

"But we're supposed to stay together! Mom said."

I choke down a groan. If I leave it here, it'll be gone by the time school gets out! "Then we'll take it with us," I say.

The chair rattles over the cracks as I push it down the sidewalk. When we get to the next crossing, I wheel it down the ramp into the street.

Then I get an Inspiration.

"You want a turn pushing?" I say to Rosie.

She blinks at me. "Um, okay."

Just as she starts to push, I hop onto the seat.

"Hey!" she says. "You're making it heavy!"

"Not too heavy for someone as strong as you," I say, making myself comfortable. "And sisters look out for each other, right?"

"But we're gonna be late," she whines.

I cross my arms. "Not if you run."

Rosie sighs and starts pushing me across the street. The chair jolts over a bump, and I grip the arms. Halfway up the ramp, we stop.

"Push harder," I say. "Come on, Rosie!"

She grunts and pushes. Slowly, the chair inches forward, bit by bit, until we're at the top. The sidewalk flattens out in front of us.

"Faster!"

We really get going then. It's bumpy, but it's *awesome*. For a block or so, I pull my legs up under me with the breeze in my face and the houses whizzing by. When I look back, Rosie is trotting along with her head down and her arms straight out in front of her.

"You're doing great," I say, because she looks like she could use a little pep talk.

"Meena?" she says, panting.

"Yeah?"

"How come Sofía gave me a bracelet but you didn't?" she asks. "Aren't we friends too?"

"We're sisters," I say. "It's different."

"Do you like Sofía more than me?"

"I like her different."

"Different in a *more* kind of way?"

"Stop talking. You're slowing us down."

We round the last corner. The sidewalk slopes down the rest of the way to school. Rosie starts to run, the chair rolling faster and faster—so fast that

Rosie lets go and chases me. I throw my head back and raise my fists in the air. "Woo-hoo!"

Finally, the sidewalk levels out again, and I coast to a stop by the bike rack.

Eli is standing there, parking his bike. He has on a red coat with white sleeves. There are pins and patches all over it, and it's so big that it hangs down over his hands.

"Isn't that Riley's jacket?" I ask.

He doesn't answer. He stares at me, a crinkle in his forehead.

I scratch the back of my neck, wondering if one of us is supposed to apologize. "Did you hear from him?" I ask finally.

He reaches his hands out of his sleeves and grabs the straps of his backpack. "He's coming home Friday."

I nod. "So you can still do your concert."

"Yep." He squints at me then. "You okay?"

It takes me a second before I understand why he's asking. The seizure! I wave my hand in the air. "I'm fine."

Eli gives a slight nod. I bounce my heel against the sidewalk. His eyes flick to the chair and back to me. Finally, the corner of his mouth twitches. "Bulk trash day?"

I hop up, grinning. "Can I lock it up with your bike? I don't want anyone to steal it."

He full-on smirks now. "Sure." He loops the metal cord around the neck of the chair, through his tire, and around the rack. "Did you get a turn, Rosie," he asks, "or did she make you push her all the way here?"

She bounces on her toes. "It was like pushing a wheelchair!"

Eli laughs and starts heading for the playground.

"No, it wasn't!" I hiss, loud enough for him to hear. "It was like one of those thrones that servants carry so their rulers don't have to walk."

"You're not my ruler," Rosie says, hands on her hips.

"I'm your big sister. It's the same thing."

"Is not."

"Is too. I look out for you on the way to school, don't I?"

I try to take her hand, but Rosie yanks it away. "We look out for each other," she says. Before I can grab her, she runs to the entrance, pulls the glass door shut, and sticks out her tongue.

No way am I letting her be my sidekick now.

"Meena!"

I barely turn around before Sofía runs up and slams me with a hug.

"Ooof! What the heck?"

"Are you okay?" She squeezes me hard then

pulls back and checks me over. "I tried to talk to you, but you couldn't hear me. Then I tried to call you after school, but your mom said you were asleep."

"I'm fine," I say, wriggling out of her grip.

"I've seen those little seizures where you space out," she says, "but I didn't know the big ones were so"—she takes a breath—"*big*."

"Did everybody see it?" I ask.

"Until they made us leave."

"Mom says you got to finish lunch in the *class-room*."

Sofía bites her lip. "Nobody really felt like eating."

I nod, remembering. "Salisbury steak."

"No, it was just—" She shakes her head. "It was scary, Meena."

I don't know what to say to that. I rock back on my heels. "Well, everything's okay," I say. Now that I have my Ring back, I shouldn't have to worry about having a seizure.

Sofía wrinkles her forehead at me. "You're sure you're all right?"

"I'm fine!" I say, throwing back my shoulders. "I'll even race you to the swings."

I take off running. My backpack bounces against my shoulders. Sofía's feet pound against the sidewalk behind me. When we round the corner, and the soccer field opens up in front of us,

I shoot past the Taylor twins throwing a football and the fifth-grade girls standing in a circle, shuffling their feet.

I'm about to tear across the grass when the bell rings, so I change directions and run for the door instead. With my super speed, I'm the first one there! Sofía catches up and stands next to me, panting. The playground empties as kids hurry toward us to line up, noisy and laughing, filling the space around us.

Then something strange happens.

Aiden sees me and stops short. Maddy bumps into him from behind. Lin slows down and stares.

The noise dies down. The laughing stops. Aiden nudges Maddy, who whispers to Lin, who's already elbowing Pedro.

None of them get into the line.

I turn and face the first graders. I give a little wave to the girl I saved, but she winces and hides behind her friend. When the playground monitor calls her class inside, they duck their heads and scurry past without looking at me.

What's going on? All last week, kids picked me for their teams. They sat by me at lunch. Why are they acting like they're scared of me now?

Is this because of my seizure? But that didn't count! I wasn't wearing my Ring!

Eli is the last to arrive, bouncing a basketball

in his too-big jacket. Pedro tugs on his floppy sleeve and whispers. Eli bends his head to listen, then raises his eyebrows at me.

I feel my cheeks getting hot. I look at Sofía. Something fierce comes over her face.

She steps closer to me, standing so close that our shoulders are touching. She crosses her arms and sticks out her chin, daring everyone with her eyes.

Eli hugs the ball to his chest and moves to stand next to her. One by one, the other third graders get into line behind them.

When the playground monitor calls our class, I turn and lead the way inside.

I don't check to see if anyone follows.

12

My whole class avoids me all day. When I try to join in for kickball at morning recess, everyone suddenly decides to go play soccer instead. When Nora and Maddy see that the only lunch seats left are next to mine, they stand there shifting from foot to foot until Sofía smacks her apple juice down on the table and snaps, "She's not contagious."

They sit down. By the time I've finished my tater tots, they're stealing glances. When I'm done, Nora springs up and says, "I can take your tray." She whisks it away before I can answer. On my way out, Maddy rushes to open the door for me like she thinks I can't do it myself.

I liked it better when they were scared of me.

Sofía is the only one who acts normal. Except for Eli, who just unlocks my chair at the end of the day and says, "See you," like usual, before riding away.

I wish Rosie were here to push me. I turn my

chair around and kick it like a gym scooter, holding on to the seat and rolling myself backward down the sidewalk. Halfway home, I park under the tree where the mattress was leaning this morning and sit there spinning, staring up through the leaves for a while, wondering how everything can change so fast. Last week, everyone acted like I was one of a kind—like the Ring made me different from them. Now they're acting like having seizures does.

I don't want to be that kind of different.

What did they see, anyway? What could be bad enough to make them forget how I saved that girl and clipped to the top of the chart and even won elimination?

I wheel the rest of the way home and park my chair behind the garage where Mom won't see it right away. "There you are," she says when I walk through the door. "I was about to go looking for you."

I shrug off my backpack and turn to face her. "I want to see what a seizure looks like."

She glances up from her computer.

"Everyone knows but me," I say, "even the kids in my class." I stand up straighter. "I want to know what they saw."

Mom takes off her glasses and sets them on the table. "You might not like it, honey."

"I don't care."

She twists the end of her ponytail around her finger and lets it go. "I could look for a video," she says, "but I'm not sure what's out there. Could I describe it to you instead?"

"You've already done that. I want to *see* it."

Finally, she sighs and puts her glasses back on. "Let me see what I can find." I kick off my shoes and step up to the table while she clicks. After a minute, she holds out her arm and pulls me in close. "Let's try this one."

It's a video called "Absence Seizures in Children." It's pretty boring, actually. It's just a bunch of kids staring into space, one after another.

But then I start to notice something. All the clips look alike. Not the kids. They're all different sizes and shapes and colors. It's their expression that's the same. Their faces are blank and still. Their eyes are empty, like someone turned out the lights inside their bodies. They stay like that for a minute, then they blink, and it's like the light goes back on again.

When the video ends, I stare at the frozen screen and swallow down a shiver in my throat. "Is that what I look like when I space out?"

"Pretty much," Mom says.

"What about the other kind? Like in the lunchroom."

"It's called a convulsive seizure."

"Can you show me one of those?"

Mom tucks a lock of hair behind my ear without meeting my eyes. "I can understand why you'd want to see that, Meena, but . . ." She closes the computer. "I need to think about it, okay?"

I stiffen. It must be bad if she won't show me.

She squeezes my arm. "I talked to your doctor today."

"Doctor Suri?"

"No, your neurologist."

"The guy with the fish tank in his office?"

"That's the one."

The last time I saw him was after my EEG—this weird test where they put wires all over my head and made me look at flashing lights and blow on a pinwheel until I was out of breath. They even kept me hooked up to the machine while I took a nap in the office. "What did he want?" I ask.

"He thinks it's time for you to start taking medication to prevent your seizures."

I pull away from her. "You mean a shot?"

"Not a shot," she says. "Just a pill. You'll take it twice a day."

"For how long?"

"For as long as you need it."

When I come downstairs for dinner, there's a brown bottle next to my plate. My name is on the label, above a word so long it looks like it's written in code. I try to open it, but the lid just spins.

"It's childproof," Dad says.

That should be no match for my super strength!

But Dad reaches across the table, pops the bottle open, and taps out a pill.

It looks like a little blue submarine. I sigh and gulp it down. At least I'll be eating something blue every day. I wish it were purple.

All through dinner, I think about superheroes. I wonder if they ever mind being different from everyone else. It must get kind of lonely. After all, Superman got dumped on earth all alone. Wonder Woman left her island to fight evil. Spider-Man never really fit in with people *or* with spiders. Even when superheroes hang out together, they all have different powers, so they aren't even like *each other*.

When we finish eating, I help Dad with the dishes while Mom puts Rosie to bed. "Do you still have your old comic books?" I ask, drying the last plate and handing it to him.

He stacks it in the cabinet. "If your mom didn't throw them out in a burst of tidying."

"Can I see them?"

"Really? You're interested in those?"

"Sure."

He narrows his eyes at me. "You're not going to

cut them up, are you? Like you did with my running magazines?"

"I was making you a motivational collage!"

"Yeah, well, it motivated me to cancel my subscription."

"So I saved you money, too," I point out. "I just want to read them."

He brightens. "Okay, then." I follow him into the garage and watch while he sets up a stepladder and climbs up to a high shelf. "Last I knew," he says, "they were right about . . . Here they are!"

He grunts, lifts down a big plastic bin, and sets it on the floor. The lid is gritty, but when I pry it off, I see stacks of comic books, each in its own plastic sleeve.

"Do you have any Wonder Woman?" I ask, rummaging through the stack.

"Nah, I never really read DC. I've got Spider-Man, Iron Man, Hulk. . . ." He holds one up. "This one's even autographed. Limited edition. Only one thousand signed."

"Where'd you get it?"

"Your mom bought it for me when we were dating."

"Mom liked comic books?"

"No, but she liked me." He wags his eyebrows. "I was quite a catch."

I make a gagging sound and grab the comic on top of the stack.

"Here," Dad says. He spreads a tarp on the cement, and we sit with our backs against the side of the car. For a while, we page through comic books by the yellow light of the bulb hanging from the rafters, breathing in the faint smell of grass clippings and gasoline. I study the different kinds of superpowers. I examine the colorful costumes. After a while, I notice something.

I turn a few more pages. I rifle through the bin of comics, checking the covers. "Why aren't there any girls in these things?"

"There are some," Dad says. He looks up from a comic with a black-suited Spider-Man on the cover. "Not enough, though." He digs into the bin and hands me another book. "Here's one. Have you heard of Firestar?"

I shake my head. The woman on the cover has long, red hair and a matching mask. She's surrounded by a blast of fire, like the blank figure on my movie poster surrounded by a ring of rainbow. But her squeezy-tight suit is so close to skin color that she almost looks naked. Plus, she has on high-heeled boots!

She *must* have superpowers to be able to move around in those things.

"Why is she dressed like that?" I ask.

Dad cringes. "Yeah, it's not very practical. On the other hand, she can manipulate microwave radiation, so she has that going for her."

"Can she fly?" I ask.

"Yep."

Maybe the heels don't bother her when she's in the air. Still. I glance at my orange sneakers. Good traction. Bright color. *Those* are the kind of shoes a superhero should wear. "What else can she do?"

"Throw fireballs. Generate extreme heat," Dad says. "The only problem is that she's not actually immune to the effects of radiation. She can manipulate it, but later in the series she actually gets sick from exposure to her own power. It's a pretty cool twist."

I stare at him. "I thought you couldn't hurt a superhero."

"You can if you know their weakness," he says. "Every superhero has one."

"They do?"

"Sure. Electro can't get wet. Daredevil is sensitive to noise. Spider-Man runs out of webs sometimes. It'd be boring otherwise."

"Does Superman have a weakness?" I ask.

"The most famous one of all. It's called kryptonite. It takes away his powers."

"Oh, yeah." I forgot all about that. I think for a minute. "What do you call the opposite?"

"The opposite of kryptonite?"

"No, I mean . . . Let's say you have a special object that *gives* you your power. What do you call that?"

"Oh, you mean an amulet. Or no, wait. That just protects you. If it has powers, I think it's called a talisman. Most superheroes don't have those, though. Their powers are sort of built-in."

Huh. I trace the shape of the Ring through my shirt. So that's what this is: a talisman. I tilt my head and look at Dad, impressed. "How do you know all this stuff?"

He crosses his ankles in front of him and opens Spider-Man again. "Countless hours of wasted youth."

I stare at the bin of comic books. More than ever, I want to know what the Ring can do.

I mean, mind-controlling my little sister is okay, but it's not *enough*.

My classmates are scared of me. Mom wants to watch over me. My doctor thinks I need a pill. They all think I'm the one who needs saving.

But the superheroes in these comics can do more than I imagined—things I never thought to test. They can move things without touching them. They can see the future and control the weather.

They can turn invisible, pull trees out of the ground, and shoot lasers from their eyes.

Maybe I can do some of those things too.

I just need an Inspiration.

I grab a new stack of comics, lie down on my stomach, and start at the top.

13

The next morning, I walk right past kids playing kickball, Sofía playing four square, and first graders running to hide in the tube slide when they see me coming.

I have a whole *bunch* of new powers to try out—and if anyone happens to see me cause an earthquake or transport across the soccer field in the blink of an eye, so what?

That'd show them.

I head to the blacktop and look up at the basketball hoop. Pedro and Eli wouldn't be too happy if I yanked it right out of the ground, so I put my hands against the cold metal pole and try to bend it instead. Nothing. I push harder. Nope. I roll up my sleeves and give it all I've got, straining my feet against the pavement until my arms start to shake. It doesn't budge.

Okay, so I don't have super strength.

Maybe I can turn invisible!

Pedro is dribbling toward me. I stand under

the basket and imagine my body dissolving into fizz, the tiny bubbles floating into the air. I concentrate so hard that my fingers start to tingle.

Pedro looks confused. I hold my breath so he can't hear me.

"You're right in the middle of the court," he says.

"Oh. Sorry." I tuck my chin to my chest and slink away.

So I can't turn invisible, either. Big deal. Neither can Firestar.

Maybe I can manipulate radiation!

I'm a little nervous about starting a wildfire with my extreme heat since Hydro-Man isn't here to blast water out of his body, but whatever. These kids know how to stop, drop, and roll.

I stand at the edge of the soccer field and try turning myself into a roaring fireball. I open my arms, summoning heat from within, feeling it build, imagining it radiating outward until—*BLAST!*

Nothing happens.

When the bell rings, I shuffle into the building behind everyone else.

The rest of the morning, I try to predict what will be on the lunch menu. I attempt to operate the pencil sharpener from across the room. I stare out the window, trying to make the sun cloud over.

Nothing works.

"I don't get it," I whisper to Sofía at lunch. "I

should be able to do *something* besides mind control by now." I open my container of grapes and offer them to her. "I mean, I guess I have superhuman reflexes, too, because I saved that girl. But still."

Sofía spreads a few potato chips on her sandwich and then hands me the bag.

"Maybe I should just concentrate on developing my brain powers." I crunch into a chip. "I mean, it'd be great if I could make the earth stop rotating or summon a magical weapon or whatever, but it's not like Firestar got to pick her powers." I let out a big sigh. "Maybe I just have a superhuman mind."

Sofía doesn't answer. She plinks the tab off her can of apple juice and hands it across the table.

"Should I try to hypnotize someone?" I ask, sticking the tab in my pocket. "Or practice reading minds some more? Do you think I have to be touching the person for it to work? Because that'd explain why—"

"Meena."

"Yeah?" I take a swig of milk.

She's moving her jaw back and forth again. "Do you think maybe—"

"Hey, you guys!" Eli bangs his tray down next to us. "I think I got it!"

Oh, no.

He puts one knee on the bench, pushes his

hand out of Riley's floppy jacket sleeve, and sticks his palm into his other armpit. "Listen."

"Can't you save it for the concert?" I ask.

"What? No," Sofía says. "That's just for your family. I won't get to see it." She turns back to Eli. "Go ahead."

He starts pumping his elbow up and down. At first, the only sound is a couple of Riley's medals clinking together.

Then these awful squeaky noises come out of the jacket.

Sofía watches, her eyes dancing. When he's finished, she claps like crazy. "Your brother is gonna love that."

Eli plops down on the bench and gives her a shy smile. "Does it really sound like farting?"

"Mostly," Sofía says. "Sometimes it's more like sneakers on the gym floor."

"But I'm on the right track?"

"Definitely."

He grins. "Yeah, okay. I'll keep working on it." He picks up a french fry and glances at me. "What do you think?"

I roll my eyes. "I think you're wasting your time."

Eli stops dragging his fry through ketchup and stares at me. "Why?"

"Riley's not here to see it," I say, the back of my neck getting hot. "He's never here."

Eli shrugs. "He'll be here this weekend."

"You really think so?" My fingers tighten around a carrot stick.

"Duh," Eli says. "He *said* so. And he's my *brother*."

I snap my carrot in two. "Well, he sure doesn't act like it."

Sofía gasps. "Meena!"

"What's that supposed to mean?" Eli asks.

"It means he never paid attention to you before," I say. "Why would he start now?"

Eli gapes at me, his face getting red. "He *is* coming. You'll see. And I'm gonna show him my sound effects, and he'll take me to the pool, and he'll probably start teaching me the butterfly stroke too, because he's one of the best swimmers in the world. You see this?" Eli stands and points at a big letter stitched to the front of the jacket. "Riley got it for being on varsity." He points to a patch on the shoulder. "And he got this because he was All-Conference." He points to a pin. "And this is because he was first in his division."

I cross my arms. "Well, if he's so great, then where is he?"

Eli grabs the edge of the table and leans across until his face is right in mine. "He's *coming*."

I don't say anything. Because I don't believe it.

Maybe the Ring lets me see into the future.

Eli picks up his tray and stalks off.

"Eli!" Sofía calls after him. When he doesn't stop, she turns to me, her eyes blazing. "You want to be a hero?" she says. "Then stop acting like a villain!"

I sit up straighter. "I'm not the one who—"

But she doesn't let me finish. She just picks up her lunch and follows Eli, leaving me at the table alone.

I try to make up with Eli and Sofía all day.

I mean, I don't actually talk to them. I use mind control.

I try telling them how sorry they are for the way they talked to me. I imagine them writing me long apology notes and passing them under the desks. I *WHOOSH* feelings of guilt and regret at them.

Nothing works. Not one thing. It's almost like I don't even *have* any powers.

But I know I do! I saved that girl, didn't I? I mind-controlled Rosie over and over.

I'll prove it.

The next day, I am *extra* helpful at school. When it's time for the Homework Handler to do her job, I grab the vocabulary sheets from her and do it myself. When Pedro raises his hand in science, I blurt out the answer so he won't get it wrong. When Lin trips and lands on the floor, I knock over the whole art cart on my way to help her up.

Nobody seems to appreciate it. Mrs. D even clips me down!

I'm so frustrated that night that I can't focus on my homework. It's easy math, dividing by one hundred, but all I can do is sit at the kitchen table kicking my feet against the chair and staring at the zeros—all those empty circles on the page.

I finger the empty hole of the Rainbow Ring.

I remember the empty eyes of the seizure kids.

I think about the empty spot on my hero poster, the rainbow colors spreading out from nothing at all.

I lay my head on the table. I don't get it! Everything was fine after I found the Ring. I saved that girl. I mind-controlled Rosie. I helped everyone in my class. I was strong and fierce and powerful—like nobody else in the world!

Then I lost the Ring, and I couldn't save Eli at the pool. And I had a seizure.

Now that I have the Ring again, everything should be fine! But it isn't. Nothing is back to the way it was before. It's almost like something is blocking my powers.

Hang on.

I sit up again and spot the brown pill bottle in the middle of the table. I pick it up.

The Ring was working. Then I started taking this, and zip. Zero. Nothing.

What if the medication is my kryptonite?

I drop the bottle and scrape my chair back. The pills aren't helping me. They're blocking my powers, like a wet blanket over a flame.

But I don't need them! Superheroes don't take medicine, and they don't have seizures.

Maybe that's why I found the Ring. I bet it chose me so I wouldn't have epilepsy anymore—so I could be stronger and more powerful than anybody.

I just have to stop taking these pills.

M eena Zee, report to the office, please."

At the sound of the intercom, everybody turns to look at me. I glance at the clip chart in the front of the room, but I'm nowhere near Go to the Principal.

"Go ahead, Meena," Mrs. D says.

I head into the hallway, feeling a little shaky. Voices filter through each door as I tiptoe past the other classrooms. When I reach the office, Mom is standing by the main desk.

"What are you doing here?" I ask.

"You forgot this." She holds out the blue pill I left by my cereal bowl.

"Oh." I shift from one foot to the other. "Sorry."

But I'm not. Last night, I pretended to swallow my pill. I slipped it into my pocket, took it up to my workshop, and stuck it through the slot of my piggy bank.

This morning, instead of faking it, I "forgot" the pill next to my bowl.

So much for that.

"Is Sofía coming over after school?" Mom asks, dropping the pill into my hand.

It's my turn to have her over, but we haven't talked since she blew up at me the other day. "Um . . ." I rock back on my heels. "We might stay on the playground for a while, if that's okay."

"As long as you're together." She kisses me on top of my head. "I'll let her mom know."

I head back into the hallway. When I look over my shoulder, Mom is still watching me through the glass door. I stop at the drinking fountain, pretend to toss the pill into my mouth, and take a long drink of water.

I stick the pill in my pocket once she's out of view.

"I told my mom that we're going to the playground after school," I tell Sofía at lunch. "But if you don't want to, you can go home and tell your mom we changed our minds."

Sofía peers across the table at me. "Are you saying you don't want me to stay?"

I shrug. "I'm saying you should do what you want."

She crosses her arms. "Then I'll stay."

"Fine," I say.

"Fine."

I pick the seeds out of my good-for-you sandwich bread. She opens her bag of Flaming Crunchers. Her flower headband is blue today. She slips it off, then slides it back into place.

"I'm staying in for recess to do math," she says after a minute, "but if you don't want to, you can still go out."

"Are you saying you don't want me there?"

"I'm saying you should do what you want."

I cross my arms. "Then I'll stay."

"Fine," she says.

"Fine."

We stare at each other for a few more seconds then drop our eyes. I'm biting into my sandwich when I hear a plink. She slides her can tab across the table and leaves it next to my milk. I chew a while longer before I reach over, pick it up, and slip it into my pocket.

So at least that's settled.

The rest of the day, we aren't exactly friendly, but at least we aren't fighting. She works on math after lunch while I work on handwriting. At last recess, she plays horses with Nora while I get in line for double Dutch. The rope twirlers exchange a look when it's my turn to jump, but at least they don't run screaming.

Eli is still ignoring me, but he's in a good mood—drumming pencils on his desk, making heavy metal sounds with his mouth, and bobbing his head—all because Riley is finally coming home. If we *do* go to Eli's dumb concert tomorrow, and Riley ends up ignoring him, maybe I *won't* try to mind-control him into feeling better.

When the last bell rings, I head to my cubby and cram everything into my bag while Sofía takes her time packing up. "Meet you outside?" I ask.

She nods, and I head to the playground.

For a few minutes, I wait inside the tube slide, listening for the bus to rumble away. I leave my backpack and climb out again. The line of cars by the school is gone now, the playground empty. Finally, I have it all to myself.

It's time to find out if I can fly.

It's been more than twenty-four hours since my last pill. That should be enough to restore my powers.

I want this one more than any of them. It would prove that the Ring works—that it keeps me safe and makes me strong. If I can fly, then I'm not just some kid who has seizures. I'm someone who can help Eli and look out for Rosie—someone worth having as a best friend.

I plant my feet at the edge of the soccer field. That's plenty of room for a running start. I put my head down and scuff my feet through the grass like a racehorse at the starting gate.

I take off across the field, pumping my arms, pushing myself harder and harder until I'm running so fast my feet barely touch the ground, then I spread my arms and leap!

Thud.

I land in the grass. I lick my finger and stick it up in the air to see which way the breeze is blowing. I put my head down and take off again—faster this time with the wind at my back, blasting across the field until I spread my arms again to leap and—

Thud.

I stand with my hands on my knees, panting. This has to work. It *has* to!

Maybe I need to get higher.

I jog back and climb the platform of the zip line. I grab the handle, push off, and zip across. Then I let go and—

Thud.

I clamber on top of the tube slide next. This time, I try using magic words before I jump. "Cookie cupcake blastoff—"

Thud.

I sink down onto my knees and pound my fists on the ground. I want to fly! I *need* to!

But what if I can't?

Or maybe . . .

I turn and face the swings.

I need to launch myself.

I brush wood chips off my knees and storm across the playground, my jaw set. I sit on a swing and pump my legs, pulling hard on the chains, climbing higher. In a minute, I'm soaring so high that I hang in midair for a split second before the chains go slack and the swing starts to drop again.

I'm breathing fast now, my chest squeezing tight. I've never jumped from this high. The air swishes in my face, then against my back. The Ring

presses into my chest, then lifts away. I take a deep breath, pull the swing to the tippy top—

"Cookie cupcake blastoff!"

I arc through the air like I weigh nothing at all, soaring, the wind whistling by.

I'm flying!

THUD!

Pain shoots up my knees as I smack against the ground and tumble forward, slamming my elbow and landing on my shoulder, hard.

"Meena!"

I can't breathe . . . I clutch my elbow and roll onto my back.

"Oh my gosh, are you okay?"

Sofía is above me. I try pushing off the ground, but pain zings up my whole arm. "I'm fine," I say, gasping for air.

"What happened?"

"I fell off the swing."

She drops her backpack and kneels down beside me. "Can you get up?"

I roll onto my side and moan, pulling my knees to my chest.

Sofía springs to her feet. "I'm getting help."

"No!" I force myself to sit up. My whole body feels like it's exploding. "I'm fine," I say through gritted teeth. I squeeze my eyes shut, my shoulder throbbing.

Sofía kneels again. "You must have spaced out," she says.

"What?" My eyes flick back open.

"That must be why you let go."

I can't believe my ears. "That's what you think?"

"Well, do you remember anything?"

"Of course I remember," I snap. "I just lost my grip. I don't *have* seizures anymore."

Sofía sits back on her knees. "What do you mean, you don't have them?"

I pull the Ring out of my shirt. "This keeps me safe. That's why I found it!"

She stares at me.

"What?" I say, getting annoyed.

She looks at the swing, still swaying in the air, then back at me. "You didn't fall," she says quietly. "You jumped."

I stand up, wincing, my knees screaming at me.

"Why would you do that?" she demands.

I try to brush the wood chips off my legs, but my hands are scraped up and stinging. "I wanted to see if I could fly," I mutter.

Sofía throws back her head and groans.

"What? Maybe I can!"

She glares at me. "*Did* you?"

I tug my shirt into place. "Just because I didn't, doesn't mean I can't."

Sofía crosses her arms. "You can't."

"You don't know what I can do," I hiss. "I saved that girl from a speeding van, didn't I?"

"You said it was barely moving."

"I mind-controlled Rosie."

"She does whatever you want anyway."

I hold up the Ring again. "I wasn't wearing this when I had seizures! You think that's a coincidence?"

She throws up her arms. "Yes!"

"No," I say, shaking my head, my voice getting higher. "The Ring is my talisman. It gives me powers."

Sofía's eyes are wild. "You don't have any powers, Meena."

I stagger backward. I feel like I'm alone on a crumbling island, sinking into the lake of fire, watching Sofía fly off without me.

It's only then, with the gap widening between us, that a new idea begins to dawn.

"You're jealous," I breathe.

She doesn't answer. She just sways silently before finally whispering, "Maybe."

That's it! My chest swells. "You're jealous that I have superpowers and you don't."

She takes a step back. "I'm not jealous of that!"

"Then what?"

She rears up on me. "I get to see my cousins once a year," she says. "I don't have family in town. I don't have a sister. But you . . . Eli and Rosie are like built-in friends, and you don't appreciate them. Sometimes you aren't even *nice* to them."

"That's not true," I say. "I use my powers to help them."

She puts her hands on her hips. "How?"

"I made Rosie pick—" I stop. "I got Eli to—" I stop again.

I wanted to save them. Both of them. I *tried* to save them.

Didn't I?

Flames seem to ignite in the pit of my stomach then. They rise up my throat, spread to my fingertips, and radiate through the ends of my hair. "You don't believe me," I say, clenching my jaw. "But you will."

I push past her and run for the monkey bars.

"What are you doing?" she calls.

I start climbing the ladder, imagining my whole body blazing like Firestar. "I'll show you," I yell over my shoulder. "When I fly off the top, you'll believe me then!"

"Meena, no!"

I reach for the next rung, but I feel a tug on my ankle. I try to kick free, but Sofía is hanging on with her whole body. My fingers slip from the rung, one by one, until I lose my grip, and she pulls me down.

She wraps her arms around me from behind.

I try to break away—to shoot acid out my pores or lasers out my eyes or to turn my body into a ball of fire, too hot for Sofía to hold—but nothing works.

Finally, I stop kicking and screaming and slump in her grip.

Sofía circles around in front of me. She grabs hold of my sleeves, leans in close, and tries to look me in the eye. "Meena," she says.

I yank free and run.

15

I'm sore all over when I wake up Saturday morning.

My shoulder aches when I roll over. My hands sting when I sit up and clutch the edge of my bed.

I heave an achy sigh and touch my friendship bracelet, walking my fingers over it so the beads spin slowly around my wrist, one color at a time. I pinch the one and only yellow bead and roll it between my fingers.

Sofía doesn't believe me. She still doesn't. I couldn't even convince my best friend. If she still is my best friend, I mean.

I turn and look at the paint card that's taped to the wall—that bluish purple, bright as a jewel, the only proof I have left.

Easing myself up, I test out my ankle and hobble past Rosie's empty bed. I peel the paint card off the wall and take it to my workshop. I breathe Magic Mist onto the window and draw a circle with beams shining out from it.

I make a wish. And even though it's brand-new,
I feel like it's the wish I've been making all along.

I want to be better. I don't have to be better
than anyone else. Just better than I was. Better than
I am. I close my eyes, clutching the paint card.

Please.

The door of the hardware store swishes open, but I
don't bother waving my arms to make it look like
I'm controlling it.

Everybody knows it's automatic.

I step inside and inhale the smell of mulch and
motor oil. Rosie runs to the coin machines, plugs
one with a quarter, and turns the crank. A gumball
ka-chunks down the chute. She does it again, then
opens the flap and catches both gumballs in her
hand.

"Which color do you want?" she asks, holding
them out to me.

I didn't even mind-control her.

I take the blue one and bite through the hard
shell. It's almost the size of a golfball, but when it
breaks up in my mouth, it turns into a tiny sliver of
gum. If she kept them both, she'd still have barely
enough to chew. Why would she give one to me?

"I'm going to ask about renting a tiller," Mom
says. "Rosie, do you want to come with me or stay
with Meena?"

"Stay with Meena."

I sigh. "Can I use your phone to take pictures again?"

Mom hands it to me. "I'll come find you in a few minutes."

Rosie trails after me while I wander through the side aisles. I take a close-up of a tape measure that snaps back when you let it go. I use a color filter on a pair of magnifying eyeglasses that look like spy gear. I get a good panoramic of the industrial-size bottles of You-Must-Be-Crazy Glue, but my heart isn't really in it. My brain is itchy, thinking about the purple card, and it isn't long before I stick Mom's phone in my pocket and lead Rosie to the paint department.

Standing in front of the color display, I feel a smile coming on—the first one I've had all day. Maybe my superpowers aren't big and exciting, but that doesn't mean they aren't real. Some of Dad's comic book heroes aren't so great either. Green Lantern is allergic to yellow. (Pink I could understand, but yellow?) Iron Man is nothing but a smart guy with fancy equipment, as far as I can tell. There's even a hero named Hindsight who can't do anything but regret.

I mean, regret? What good is that?

So if my only power is mind control, you know what? That's good enough for me.

It still makes me original. And it gets me a purple bedroom, too.

I take the paint card out of my pocket and show it to Rosie. "Are you ready?" I ask.

She starts bouncing on her toes. "Yeah."

I thrust my fist in the air. "To the paint counter!"

When we march up, the guy in the red apron has his back to us. I nod at Rosie and give her a little push. "Excuse me," she says.

The guy turns around, but he doesn't see us until Rosie sticks up her hand and waves. "Well, hello there, little lady," he says, leaning all the way over the counter.

"I'm not a lady," she says. "I'm a kid."

He smiles. "How can I help you?"

"I want this one," Rosie says, pointing. "It's for our room."

I glance at the card. She's pointing to the lightest color on the square—the one that's practically white.

"You mean this one." I put my finger on the bright bluish-purple strip at the other end of the card.

Rosie frowns at me. "Nuh-uh," she says. "This one." She taps the whitish square.

I let out a huffy breath. "That's not what you picked, Rosie."

"Yes, it is," she says, her voice getting higher.

"It's the one you showed me." She flips over the card and follows the words with her finger. "Summer Mist."

My stomach goes cold. My heart starts to beat faster. "I didn't show you Summer Mist." I lean over and read the name. "I showed you Storm Cloud." I flip the card and point. "*This* one."

The guy in the red apron looks back and forth between us.

"That's the one you want," I say.

"No, it isn't," she whimpers.

"Rosie . . ." I close my eyes and take a deep breath. Concentrate . . . I need to concentrate. When I look at her again, I make my voice super calm. Slow. Hypnotic, even. "You don't want Summer Mist. It's barely even a color."

She pulls her eyebrows together. "I like it," she says.

I grab the card and point to the right square. "*This* is the color you want. It's like royal robes and starry skies and those grape icy drinks Mom won't let us buy at the pool. You don't want the room to just blend in with the rest of the house. You want something that stands out—something *original*." I thrust the strip back at her.

Rosie's bottom lip starts to quiver. "Mom said I get to pick. She said it's my turn."

I pat her back. "You *do* get to pick," I say. "I'm just helping you pick the right one."

For a long time, she stares at the card in her hand.

Finally, Mom comes up from behind us, a package of paint rollers tucked under her arm. "All set?" she asks.

Rosie nods without looking up.

Mom turns to the man behind the counter. "We'll take a gallon of your store brand in eggshell."

He looks from Mom to Rosie to me, then back again. "Which color?" he asks.

The card trembles in Rosie's hand. I hold my breath, zero in on the bright bluish-purple square. *WHOOSH. This one.*

Rosie hesitates. Her shoulders slump. "This one," she says.

She holds up the card and points to Storm Cloud.

BAM! My heart soars. I almost whoop. I wish Sofía were here to see this!

Mom leans in closer. "Which one?"

Rosie hands Mom the card and taps the strip. Then she turns, scuffs her feet across the floor, and sits cross-legged under the paint chip display.

Mom turns to me, her eyes blazing. "Rosie didn't pick this."

"Of course she did," I say, smirking.

"She doesn't like bright colors."

I snort. "Well, she's wrong."

"She is not, Meena! She likes what *she* likes. She's her own person, not one of your projects."

I cross my arms. "You think I made her pick something she doesn't want?"

Mom crosses her arms right back. "That's exactly what I think."

And I can't help it. I want to jump for joy. Because I *do* have powers! I knew it!

Mom turns to the man. "I'm sorry for the trouble. Nothing today."

I drop my arms at my sides. "What?"

"If Rosie really wants this color," Mom says, "she'll still want it tomorrow."

"Fine! Wait as long as you want," I say, turning on my heel. "Her mind is made up."

I know, because I made it up for her.

I stomp down the main aisle, kick the tire of a clearance snowblower, and slam the lid of a shiny new grill. When I hear someone ask, "Can I help you?" I stalk off in the other direction.

I'm not the one who needs help!

I storm past lightbulbs and hinges and faucets, past light switches and electrical tape, past clear drawers full of different-size nails and screws and bolts—

I stop.

For a long minute, I stand there frozen, staring straight ahead, not breathing, not looking to the side, wanting to undo what I just saw.

Then slowly, very slowly, I turn my head.

There, next to drawers full of wood screws and hexagonal nuts and crisscross bolts, is a small, clear bin with a black-and-white label.

Rainbow washers, it says.

My hand shakes as I reach over, pull it open, and plunge my fingers inside. The cold metal bits clink against one another. I scoop up a handful and stare down at them.

My Ring. My Rainbow Ring. The source of my powers. The thing that makes me different from everyone.

The whole drawer is full of them. Hundreds of them.

They're forty-five cents each.

I fling them at the floor.

They bounce and ping against the concrete as I run down the main aisle, past the machines of hollow gumballs, past the swishing doors that open by themselves, away from all those identical rings making all the same ordinary plinks behind me.

16

I slam the door to my workshop, take off my Rainbow Ring, and hurl it against the wall.

It hits my superhero poster—the hollow figure surrounded by rainbow beams. I tear it down and crumple it. I'm never drawing a suit on this thing. Never! What's the point? There's nobody there!

I don't need a cape, because I can't fly. I don't need goggles or boots, because I don't have X-ray vision or super speed. I can't control anyone with my mind, either. And it's not because of my medicine.

It's because I'm not a superhero.

I kick my helmet across the rug, tie my cape into knots, and slingshot my mask against the door. When I drop to my knees, Mom's phone slips out of my back pocket and thumps against the floor.

I stare at it for a few seconds then grab it and flick on the screen.

It only takes a minute to find what I'm looking

for. Some of the videos have titles like "What to do in case of a seizure." Others are posted with people's names, like "Tyrone having a seizure." I press the one at the top.

It's a teenage girl, her hair in a ponytail. She's lying on the floor, her arms and legs paddling the air, like she's trying to run away. She looks scared, her eyes wide open, like she can't believe what's happening to her.

She makes a strangled sound in the back of her throat.

Is she choking?

I sit up on my knees, my heart racing. Isn't anybody going to help her? Someone offscreen puts a hand on her shoulder, holding her on her side, but they don't do anything else. They just sit there, watching.

Why doesn't somebody stop her? *Why are they still recording this?*

The girl growls next, her head back, her mouth open. Her eyes keep staring, but her face is twitching now, her arms still pumping, like one of those motorized Halloween zombies.

Finally, her arms and legs slow down. Her eyes close. The person next to her rubs the girl's arm, the way you'd pet a dog. She lies still then, breathing deeply, like she's gone to sleep on the floor.

The video stops.

My breath catches in my chest, and I realize I'm crying. I let out a sob and curl up on the floor, clutching the phone tight. Even when I squeeze my eyes shut, I can't stop picturing *myself* in the video, arms flailing, face frozen in fear.

"Meena?"

Mom! She's opening the door. I sit up and tuck the phone under me.

"Do you still have my—" She stops when she sees. "What's going on?"

"Nothing," I say, smearing away tears.

She pulls the door closed and sits in front of me. "Is this about the paint?"

I swallow and shake my head.

"What, then?"

Her phone pings.

I stiffen. Mom tilts her head at me, her eyebrows drawing together. She holds out her hand.

Slowly, I reach under my leg and give her the phone.

She swipes it on. I see the faint glow of the screen reflected in her eyes before she blinks fast and looks right at me.

I tuck my chin into my chest and hug my legs. I hear the video play again. When the girl starts making that choking sound, I put my arms over my ears, pressing my forehead to my knees, making myself into a tight little ball until I think it must be over.

When I peek again, Mom is biting her lip. She lowers the phone.

"Is that what everybody saw?" I ask. "Is that what I look like when it happens to me?"

Mom cringes at the blank screen. "More or less. The teachers cleared the lunchroom as fast as they could, but yes." She meets my eyes. "That's what everyone saw."

"She looked scared," I say. "The girl in the video. Was she?"

"No. She didn't know it was happening. Like you didn't." Mom reaches over and rubs my arm up and down.

Like the offscreen person in the video did.

I jump to my feet and back away. I press my hands over my eyes, but I can't stop imagining that girl on the floor, and all I can think is that she didn't look as strong or as brave or as powerful as anyone else.

She looked like she needed to be saved.

No wonder Sofía doesn't believe in me. No wonder nobody comes near me.

I can't even save myself. And the Ring is just a hunk of metal. It won't help me either.

Which means that something else has to.

I lower my hands and take a deep breath. "I need to tell you something."

Mom gazes up at me. "Okay."

I hang my head. "I haven't been great about taking my medicine."

She reaches for my hand. "I know, hon. It's a new routine for all of us, but we'll get there."

I don't have to tell her anything else. That's my way out. Right there.

But I don't like the heavy feeling in my chest— like a stone sitting there, weighing me down, making it hard to breathe.

I go pick up my piggy bank and turn back to Mom. "Hold out your hands," I say.

She raises her eyebrows at me. "I don't want your money."

"Just do it."

When I turn the bank over, four little pills fall through the slot and into her palms. She stares at them.

"I haven't been taking them," I say.

She squints at me, like she doesn't understand what I'm saying. "You haven't been taking them . . . on purpose?" she asks.

Well, duh. "I thought I could take care of myself," I say.

"This is *how* you take care of yourself, Meena." Mom holds up the pills, her voice urgent. "These can help keep you safe. Don't you see that?"

"Are the seizures dangerous?" I ask.

"Not necessarily. But if they happen too often

or last too long, they can be. That's why we want to get them under control." Mom stands up and tucks a strand of hair behind my ear. "Will you help us?"

I take a shaky breath and turn to look out the window. There's no mist now, just a dried-up smear from this morning that makes everything blurry—another piece of magic that doesn't work.

I hold out my hand.

Mom gives me one of the pills. I toss it into my mouth, grab my water bottle, and wash it down. I open my hands and my mouth for her to see. "All gone," I say.

Like a baby.

Mom puts her arms around me and pulls me close. "This doesn't change anything, you know," she says. "You're still the same smart, fun, creative kid you always were. You have friends who care about you and a sister who looks up to you. You can do all the things you did before."

I nod against her shoulder. But I don't want to do the things I did before. I don't want to go back to painting all the same pictures as everybody and learning all the same songs and getting all the same answers. I don't want to go back to being just another kid. I want to do *big* things—extraordinary things!

But I can't. I never will.

Because I'm the one who needs to be saved.

17

I slip my note under Sofía's front door and knock as hard as I can, but I don't wait for anyone to answer.

If she doesn't want to talk to me, she doesn't have to. I wouldn't blame her.

But if she isn't too mad, or too sick of me, maybe she'll come to the playground like I asked in my note, so I can say I'm sorry to her face.

It seems like I'm always apologizing.

By the time my feet hit the wood chips, my cheeks are warm, and I'm out of breath from running. There's nobody here except for a little boy on the swings, singing loudly to himself while he pumps his legs higher and higher.

Like there's anything to be happy about.

I have to step over a puddle to climb into the orange slide. My backpack is still there, right where I left it yesterday. I push it out the bottom and lie down. It's the perfect size in here for someone to stretch out and stare at the seam where two sections of the tube meet. Even though you can't see the bolts that hold the slide together, you know they're there because a rusty trickle seeps down from the crack after it rains.

This same spot is also wide enough for two people to lie side by side—that is, if they're very good friends who don't mind squishing close, especially now that they're both a lot bigger than when they first started hanging out in here. The way the tube curves, it tilts you sideways so you can look each other in the eye.

But if you don't want to—if you're too ashamed of yourself—then when your friend lies down next to you, you can keep staring up at the smooth orange innards of the slide instead.

So when Sofía climbs in and lies down, I don't have to look her in the eye when I say, "You were right."

She doesn't say *I know* or *I told you so*. She doesn't even play dumb and say *About what?* She just lets me keep staring at the rusty seam.

Outside, the singing boy comes closer, but he's not too loud to drown out the sound of me saying, "I'm sorry."

The air inside the slide warms up from our breath, but the plastic is still cold against my back. Sofía turns onto her side and rests her head on her arm. "What happened?"

"It's just like you said." I sigh and finger the empty place below my neck. "I can't do one single thing a superhero can do. There's nothing special about me."

"I didn't say that." Sofía props herself up on her elbow. "I said you didn't have special powers."

I shrug. "Same thing. And you knew all along. You never believed in the Ring."

"No." She gazes at me. "But I believed in you. I still do."

I shake my head. "I can't save anyone. I never could."

Sofía is quiet. She turns onto her back so we're both staring at the top of the slide. "You saved me," she says finally.

I snort. "I couldn't even get you to be my side-kick."

"Before that," she says. "In kindergarten."

The boy outside stops singing. I turn and squint at Sofía.

"We moved away from everyone when we came here," she says. "All my cousins. The other kids I knew. That summer, I used to sit and wish for school to start so I wouldn't be alone, but then when it did . . ." She shakes her head. "I was too shy to talk to anybody. Sometimes it seemed like nobody even knew I was there."

I remember that—how quiet Sofía was at first.

She barely spoke or raised her head. I remember, because I wanted to know what color eyes she had, and I couldn't see them.

"At recess, I'd swing by myself," she says, "and after that, I'd hide in the craft center, drawing circles. I used to pretend they were holes that I could fall into and disappear." She turns to me. "Until you came along."

"Me?" I stare at her. "I didn't do anything."

"You noticed me." Sofía's lips quiver into a tiny smile.

I shake my head. "Anybody could have done that."

"But you're the only one who did." She hooks her pinky onto my bracelet. "You were my first friend here."

I shake my head. "I just wanted to play with you. It was no big deal."

"It was to me."

I don't know what to say. What I did back then shouldn't count for anything. It was nothing special. I was being my regular self, that's all.

It doesn't seem like that's good enough for her anymore.

"Then why—"Tears spring to my eyes. I take a breath and blink them back. "You never want it to be just us lately. You're always inviting other people in. It's like you're bored with me. Like I'm just *one* of your friends."

"It's not that," Sofía says, rolling the yellow bead between her fingers. "You're my best friend, Meena. But when we were fighting a few weeks ago . . . it was like I was on my own all over again. It hurts to be left out. I don't want to do that to anyone else."

I think about the bracelet she made for Rosie. About the times she invited other kids to stay in with us for recess. I think about how she kept letting Eli show us his sound effects.

Then I hear something that makes the back of my neck go cold.

It's like the squawk Eli's chickens make when you pick them up. I lock eyes with Sofía, my whole body going stiff. We sit up, scoot forward, and look out the bottom of the slide, but all I see is the empty playground and the muddy soccer field.

I hear it again and look up.

The singing boy is on the top of the monkey bars. He's lying flat on his stomach, clinging to the rungs with both arms, and staring at the ground below. He's one of those kids who holds his mouth wide open when he cries, and you think any second there's going to be this foghorn blast of a cry, but instead the blast stays inside so all you hear is a little chicken bleat when he takes a breath.

"Hey," I say, grabbing onto the edge of the slide. He's gripping the bars so tightly that his fingers are turning white. "Are you stuck?"

The boy doesn't answer. He takes a hitchy breath, his eyes wild.

"It's okay." I scramble out the tube, over the puddle. "I'm coming." I look around, thinking hard. Even if I had my Rainbow Ring, I couldn't fly up there and get him. I couldn't levitate him down or shoot a web to keep him from falling. I doubt I can even run fast enough to get help.

Sofía hops out of the slide. She doesn't have any more powers than I do, but she starts climbing the ladder anyway. "Hey, what's your name?" she asks.

He takes a shuddery breath and squeaks out, "Logan."

What's she doing? He's way too heavy for her to carry down.

"You're okay, Logan," Sofía says.

I eye the long drop to the ground—the one I would have jumped if Sofía hadn't stopped me yesterday. "But he can't get down," I say. The bottoms of my feet start to tingle as I look up.

"Sure, he can," Sofía says. "Can't you, Logan? I'll stay here with you, okay?"

His teeth are chattering, his legs shaking.

Sofía stands on the top rung of the ladder. I move to stand under him. I'm not stretchy or bouncy, but maybe I could at least break his fall.

"What grade are you in?" Sofía asks.

"First," he gasps.

What the heck is with all these first graders getting themselves into trouble?

"Did you have a leprechaun in your class this year?" Sofía asks.

He jerks his head in a quick nod.

"Was it the same one as the kindergarteners'?"

"Ours was a girl," he squeaks.

"How do you know?"

"She left us a note," he says through his chattering teeth. "Her name was Tallulah."

"Put your hand right here," Sofía says, pointing to a rung closer to her. "What else did she do?"

He reaches. "She turned the toilet water green."

"She had green *pee*?"

He bleats out a giggle. "I think so."

She taps his foot and points. "Step right here. Hey, I heard you before. You're a really good singer."

He slides his foot closer to her.

"Now swing your leg over here. What's your favorite song?"

Logan edges his feet closer to her. "'You Are My Sunshine.'"

"That's a good one," Sofía says. "Scoot over

this way. Will you sing it with me? *You are my sunshine . . .*"

He joins in, inching toward her. "*. . . my only sunshine . . .*"

"*You make me happy . . .*"

"*. . . when skies are gray.*" He swings his hips over the gap.

"*You'll never know, dear . . .*"

"*. . . how much I love you.*" His legs dangle, feet reaching the top rung.

"*Please don't take my sunshine away.*"

She climbs down in front of him, hand on his back. When he stretches his toes down far enough to skim the wood chips, Sofía says, "That's it. You can let go."

He lets go and drops to the ground.

She throws out her arms. "You did it!"

He looks up at the bars, then turns and hugs her around the stomach. He runs off, hop-skipping and starting the song over at the top of his lungs.

We watch him until he crosses the street and climbs the steps of a blue house. He turns and waves before disappearing inside.

I turn to Sofía in amazement. "You saved him," I say, breathless.

She laughs. "Stop it."

"It's true! He could have fallen. Or he could have been stuck up there forever. Or a storm might have blown in all of a sudden, and he could have been struck by lightning."

She rolls her eyes.

"Okay, maybe not that, but did you see how he looked at you? You saved him!"

"He saved himself."

I open my mouth to argue.

But she's right. She didn't do anything, really. She didn't leap. She didn't swoop in. She didn't even control his mind. "But you stayed with him," I say.

She shrugs. "That was all he needed."

And just like that, I know it was what I needed too.

I needed someone to stand by me in line. Someone to sit by me at lunch. I needed someone to treat me like my same old regular self—not better because of the Ring, not different because of the seizures, but the same. The same as before. The same as always.

I stare at Sofía. How did she know to do that? How did Eli? "You don't even have powers," I say.

"I don't need them." She raises an eyebrow and looks at me. "And neither do you."

18

All the way home, I can't stop thinking about how Sofía helped that kid.

It's what she always does, I realize, picking a yellow twist tie up from the sidewalk. She's nice to Rosie when I'm not. She listens to Eli when he's being annoying. She even let me test out my powers when she knew I didn't have any. Sofía wasn't thinking about being a hero. She wasn't thinking about herself at all.

Neither was I when I saved that girl or when I asked Sofía to play in kindergarten.

I just knew they needed help.

Dad is in the driveway when I get home. All the bikes are out, tools scattered around while he pumps up one of my tires.

"What's wrong with my bike?" I ask, winding the twist tie around the tip of my finger.

"I'm just getting it ready for the season." He puts the cap back onto the inner tube. "I thought we'd take them out for a ride tomorrow."

"Where to?"

"The scoop shop, if you give me a hand." He flips the bike upside down, sprays oil onto the chain, and turns the pedal with his hand. "You want to grab the wrench for me?"

I set down my backpack and pick up two of the tools at my feet. "Is it the pinchy thing or the wheely-deely one?"

He smirks. "The wheely-deely one. The other one is a pair of pliers."

I hand it to him and plop down on the cement. The pliers remind me of a bird beak. When I open them all the way, they look like a bird that's yawning. "Dad?"

"Mm-hmm."

"Does anybody write comics about regular people?"

He tightens a bolt next to the tire. "What do you mean?"

I close the pliers. They look tight-lipped and irritated now. "It just seems like you only hear about heroes that can fly or shoot lightning or pick up buses with their bare hands. But what about people who help little kids get down from the monkey bars? Or who cheer up their friends or pick up trash and keep their neighborhoods clean? Aren't they heroes too?"

"I think so."

"Even if they don't have suits?"

"Sure. You're talking about everyday heroes."

Everyday. Meaning ordinary—not original. I toss the pliers onto the driveway. They land next to a coffee can full of metal bolts and hooks and other hardware. On the top, I spot a couple of washers. They're exactly like mine, only smaller, and they don't have the rainbow sheen. I let out a big sigh.

Dad cocks his head at me. "What's up, boss?"

I look away from the coffee can. "I know I can't do anything really special if I have seizures. I was just hoping maybe I could do . . . I don't know . . . something *else*."

Dad lowers the wrench. "Who says you can't do anything special?"

My shoulders slump. "It's how everyone treats me now."

"How?"

"Like I need help."

Dad looks at me for a minute. He tosses the wrench onto the driveway with a clank. "Everyone needs help sometimes," he says, sitting down in front of me. "That's nothing to be ashamed of."

I make one of those shrugs that means *You're wrong, but I'm not going to argue.*

He scratches his chin with the back of his hand and leaves a streak of grease across his cheek. "Did you know that Albert Einstein had seizures?"

"Who's that?"

"Only one of the greatest scientific geniuses of all time."

Humph. "Never heard of him."

"How about Teddy Roosevelt? He was president of the United States. Have you heard of him?"

I shift a little. "Maybe."

Dad pokes me in the chest. "Well, he had seizures too. And he's not the only one. There have been Olympic athletes with epilepsy. Writers, artists, judges. You name it."

I pull my knees into my chest and wrap my arms around them. "You don't have to do this," I say quietly.

"Do what?"

"Some people just aren't that big of a deal. Just like some *things* aren't." I reach into the coffee can and hand him one of the metal rings. "Like this."

Dad blinks at it. "This?"

"It's called a washer," I mutter, resting my chin on my knees. "I don't know why, though, because it doesn't even clean stuff. It doesn't do anything."

He gazes at the ring in his hand for a long moment. "I hate to argue with you, but this is actually one powerful little doodad."

I glance up at him. "What do you mean?"

He stands and gives my bike tire a spin. "You've heard of nuts and bolts, right?" he asks.

"Yeah."

He points at the middle of my tire, where it's attached to the frame. "The bolt is the long one there. It holds the wheel onto the bike. See it?"

I nod.

"And the nut is the thing at the end that looks like a hexagon. It holds the bolt in place. But look there. See what's right next to the nut?"

When I get up and lean in closer, I can see the edge of a washer, sandwiched right there between the nut and the bike frame. "But the nut and the bolt are doing all the work," I say. "The washer is just sitting there."

"See, that's where you're wrong," Dad says. "Nuts and bolts get all the glory, but this baby helps them do their job." He flips the washer like a coin and catches it in the air.

"How?"

"Well, if a nut and a bolt press together too hard, they can damage the thing they're holding on to. They work better with a washer in between them to spread out the pressure."

"Huh."

"Or sometimes the nut comes loose from the bolt, because it doesn't have a flat surface to grip onto. You could be pedaling along and have the tire fly right off your bike! But stick a washer in there, and it creates a nice flat surface for the nut to press against, so everything stays tight."

I stick my finger in the spokes and twirl the tire around. "So the washer helps the nut and the bolt do a better job? At the thing they're already good at?"

"You got it."

I peek again at the little sliver of washer next to the wheel. "I can barely see it."

"It's not one to toot its own horn." Dad gives my bike horn a squeeze: *honk.*

I roll my eyes.

"If it's doing its job," he says, "you don't even notice it."

I nod. "It's like a superhero without a suit," I say slowly.

He grins. "An everyday hero."

Like Sofía, I think.

Maybe I could be one too—Ring or no Ring, seizures or no seizures. I could do helpful things. Invisible things. Things that don't toot my own horn.

I think I know where to start. "Can Eli ride bikes with us tomorrow?" I ask. "He could make his motorcycle sound the whole way. Or, no, wait . . ." I remember then, and my shoulders slump. "He won't want to come while Riley's home." I sigh. At least I can still cheer him on at his concert tonight, no matter how much spit he sprays.

Dad's face darkens. "Actually," he says, "your Mom talked to Aunt Kathy a little while ago. Riley didn't make it."

"What?" I take a step back. "Why not?"

"Something came up."

"Again?"

"I guess so."

My stomach squeezes. "Something more important than seeing Eli?"

"I don't know, kiddo," Dad says with a sigh. "His friends decided to stay a little longer, and he was only going to be home for a couple of days anyway, so . . ." Dad rubs the back of his neck. "He changed his plans."

"How can he do that to Eli?" I clench my fists. "Why is he *always* doing that?"

"Because nineteen-year-old college boys are not the most considerate creatures on earth."

"But he promised!" I start pacing, remembering how happy Eli was yesterday, drumming his pencils, making train sounds with his mouth. I picture him running home after school, his jacket flying open, thinking Riley would finally be there.

But he wasn't. I predicted the future.

I stomp my foot against the ground. Why couldn't I have been wrong about *that*?

"I'm going over there," I say.

Dad rests a hand on my head. "I know you

want to help, Meena, but you can't fix this."

He's right. I can't. I couldn't save Eli at the pool, and I can't change what's happening now.

But I'm going anyway. "Can I take my bike?" I ask.

Dad flips it onto its wheels. "It's all yours."

19

I grip the handles of my bike and pump the pedals as hard as I can. Soaring down the sidewalk, the wind whips my hair, and I pass by houses so fast that it almost feels like I'm flying.

I turn onto Eli's sidewalk, leaping off my bike before it stops and dumping it in the grass. The garage is open and empty, so Aunt Kathy must be out, but Eli might still be here. I knock hard on the front door and wait.

Nobody answers.

The window on the door is cut into a zillion little triangles of glass. I press my face against it and squint down the hall. A bright smudge glows from the door of Eli's room, so I know he's home, but nothing is moving—nobody loping toward me with a gerbil in one hand and a pooper scooper in the other.

I pound again. Maybe he's still ignoring me. I guess I deserve it.

Then I remember how he kept his eye on the

pool entrance that day—how he kept watching for Riley after we knew he wasn't coming.

If Eli could hear me when I first knocked, he would have come running. And if he can't hear me, then . . .

I know where he is.

I jump down from the stoop and hurry around the house. It's weird being back here by myself. It's lonely and still. I feel like I have to keep quiet for some reason, so I tiptoe through the grass, toward the back porch and the little chirping sounds of Eli's chickens. I hear a metallic rattle as one of them bangs against the side of the coop. The step creaks when I put my foot on it. I take a big breath and climb onto the porch.

Our milk jug igloo is still in the corner. It's saggy and lopsided now, mostly because we tried to move it into the yard to make room for the new chicken coop.

It turns out that thing isn't exactly portable.

I can just make out what looks like a shadowy figure inside the frosty pile of jugs. I step toward it. "Eli?" I whisper.

No answer.

I creep closer. The rotting wood planks groan under me with each tiny step. I smell the musty floorboards and the wood shavings that line the coop. One of the chickens pecks at the wire. Finally,

I'm close enough to crouch down and peer into the igloo.

Eli is sitting with his back to me, his head on his knees, cursive letters slanting across the back of his red wool jacket—Riley's jacket. The one with the pins and patches and medals that prove how great Riley is.

The jacket he left behind.

I look for a way in, but Eli is blocking the door, the igloo like a fortress.

Or maybe it's more like an island, crumbling into a lake of fire.

"Eli," I say again. It's not a question this time. It's me reaching my hand across the lake.

"What," he answers finally. It's not a question either. It's Eli, pulling up a drawbridge, staying out of reach.

"Can I come in?" I ask quietly.

He shakes his head no.

My heart squeezes in my chest. "I want to help."

"I don't want help." His voice is dull and wilted. "I don't want anything."

My hands clench. My legs twitch. I want to barge past him into the igloo. I want to pull him to safety. If he'd turn around and let me . . .

But he won't. He still doesn't want to be saved. Maybe he doesn't need to be.

I sink down onto the floor outside the igloo,

facing the other way. I tip my head up and stare at the porch ceiling—wood slats like I'm sitting on, only smaller. Tighter. Closer together.

"What can I do?" I ask.

"Nothing."

So that's what I do.

Nothing at all.

Because I'm not a hero, and I can't fix this.

All I can do is stay here by his side while the island crumbles beneath us.

I swallow hard and rest my chin on my knees. I don't say anything reassuring or *WHOOSH* any positive thoughts over to him. We just sit together, back to back. Silent.

For a long time, I close my eyes and listen to the soft clucking of the chickens and the swishing of the pine trees.

When Eli finally speaks, his voice is so quiet that I barely hear it over the sound of the breeze. "He said he'd come."

I open my eyes.

"I wanted to show him my walnut collection. And the robin's nest out back. I wanted to go to the pool and ride our bikes and work on our sound effects . . . but we didn't have to do any of those things if he didn't want to." He takes a shuddery breath. "I just wanted to see him."

"I know," I say.

I think about the last time I saw Riley, at a family dinner before he left. He spent the whole time texting his friends. Whenever he did look up, he was wearing mirrored sunglasses that made him look like he was closed for business.

I wonder if he's a good brother. Because I know Eli is. He'd do anything for Riley.

"Why doesn't he do what he says he will?" Eli asks.

I sigh. "He was probably having such a good time that he didn't think about you."

"That's even worse," Eli says.

He's right. It's worse not to be thought of.

I do that sometimes, though. I forget to think about other people. I did it to Eli when he tried to show me his sound effects. I did it to Sofía when she kept asking to play four square. I did it to Rosie when she wanted to make bracelets.

I do it to Rosie all the time.

Sure, I let her hang around, if I'm in the mood and if she's not in my way. I'm not really thinking of her, though. And isn't that the worst thing of all?

I wonder if I'm a good sister. Because I know Rosie is. She'd do anything for me.

What would I do for her?

"Why didn't he want to see me?" Eli asks.

I swallow hard. "Maybe because he knows you'll always be here," I say, "because you always have been. I know he's your hero, Eli, but he isn't perfect." I let out a big breath. "Nobody is."

One of the chickens flutters inside the coop. I watch her stretch out her wings and then tuck them back in. Eli has gotten so many new animals this year—more than he ever had before. He takes them in and takes care of them. He plays with them and pays attention to them. He lets them know they're wanted.

I wish Riley would do that for him. Somebody should.

"Eli?"

He doesn't answer.

I look over my shoulder at him. "Can I see your walnut collection?"

For a minute, he doesn't say anything. Then he does one of those wavy shrugs that doesn't mean no. "Okay," he says.

When he turns around, there are streaks on his face where I can tell his tears dried. He reaches into the pocket of Riley's jacket and sets a walnut in between us. He pushes it across the floor, out the door to me.

"I found this one last fall. It was still in its husk, but I peeled it off."

I pick it up and admire the wrinkly brown shell.

He digs into his pocket and takes out another one. "This one still has teeth marks in it." He points to the tiny scratches. "A squirrel dropped it when he saw me coming."

"Huh." I squint at it and nod.

He fumbles in his pocket again. When he lowers his head, I can see a freckle on his scalp, right at the spot where his hair sticks straight up.

He sets another walnut in front of me. "This one is cool because it looks like a grandpa."

I pick it up and turn it over. It looks exactly like the other two.

He keeps handing me nuts. To Eli, each one is unique. I take my time examining them, listening to their stories, learning about where he found them and what makes each one different from all the others.

But I'm not really thinking about them.

I'm thinking about how Eli shares his favorite chips with me at lunch because he knows they're my favorite too. How he chained my chair to the bike rack even after our fight at the pool. How he stood by me in line with Sofía when nobody else would come near.

I'm also watching the tips of Eli's ears turn pink while he talks. I'm listening to the bounce come back into his voice and seeing the light come back into his eyes.

"Eli?" I say.

"Yeah?"

I hand back his last walnut. "I know we don't get to pick our brothers and sisters, but if we did, I'd want you to be mine."

He freezes. For a few seconds, he stares at me.

Then his whole face collapses. "What the heck, Meena?" he groans.

I blink. "What?"

A big shudder starts in the middle of his chest and rattles through his body, right to the ends of his floppy white sleeves. "I'm *glad* I don't have a sister if they go around saying stuff like that!"

"Hey!" I slug him in the shoulder. "I was trying to be nice."

He snorts. "Well, stop it."

I cross my arms. "Fine. I *was* going to ask you to show me your armpit farts, but—"

"Really?" His face brightens. "Because I'm getting pretty good."

I stick my chin out. "Prove it."

So he does.

Boy, does he.

He squeaks out a full minute of them. He does his drop-of-water cheek flick next. After that, he chugs out a helicopter sound that sprays so much spit I have to cover my face with my arms.

It's a whole concert.

When he's finished, he beams at me, wiping spit on Riley's sleeve.

"That's awesome, Eli," I say, and I mean it.

All this time, while I was working on super-powers I didn't have, he was getting good at something that was all his own—something original.

"Now teach me how to burp the ABCs," I say.

He grins.

Then he backs away from the igloo door so I can scootch inside.

20

BAM!

I jump in front of the automatic door outside the hardware store.

WHOOSH!

I spread my arms wide as it opens.

"Get inside!" I say over my shoulder. "Can't . . . hold it . . . long!"

Mom leads Rosie into the store.

POW!

I leap inside, whirl around, and wave my arms back together as the door closes. "We made it!" I gasp.

Rosie giggles. We stop and wiggle our feet on the mat of rubbery prickles then run for the gumball machines. I dig around inside my pocket. I helped Eli clean cages yesterday, so I have my own quarters this time, but I brought the washer, too. I still might see if it fits in one of the machines. Before I decide what I want, Rosie plugs two coins of her own. She lets the gumballs fall into her hand and holds them out to me. "Want one?" she asks, gazing up at me with big brown eyes.

I pick the orange gumball and leave the pink one for her. "Thanks," I say, popping it into my mouth. It only tastes like gum for five seconds, but it was still nice of her. I turn to Mom and rock back on my heels. "If you want, you can go get your garden stuff first," I say.

She raises her eyebrows at me. "Oh, can I?"

"Sure. We'll just be in the paint department." I bat my eyelashes.

She narrows her eyes and points at me. "No funny business."

I trace an *X* over my heart and grab Rosie's hand. "Come on, squirt," I say, dragging her down the aisle.

Standing in front of the bay of colors is even better when you're actually there to pick one out, not just stuffing your pockets full of cards, which seems to bug the staff, even though they're *free*.

I soak up the colors for a minute, breathing in the whole rainbow. "Are you excited?" I ask, glancing down at Rosie. "We get to wake up to a new color tomorrow!"

Rosie shrugs. "I guess."

"What do you mean, you *guess*?"

She sighs and unclips her little pink purse then and pulls out the paint card.

I take a good look at her, standing there in her little pink shoes, her hair tied up with little pink ribbons like a girl in an old storybook. Sofía is right. I don't need to use mind control to make Rosie pick what I want. She'd do anything for me.

I turn back to the display—to the hundreds of shades that aren't mine.

"You know," I say, "I'm not sure you picked the right color."

She frowns up at me. "I didn't?"

I slide the card out of her hand. "I'm a little worried about it."

"Why?"

"Well . . ." I take one last look at that beautiful bluish-purple card. Then I pull my eyes away and look at Rosie instead. "It's kind of bright, isn't it?"

She stares up at me. "It's very bright."

"And it's called Storm Cloud," I say. "Is that what you want to think about every morning? Maybe it'd be better to wake up to something with a little more sunshine in it. What do you think?"

She blinks. "Me?"

"Yeah, you. What would you pick? If it were up to you."

"It *is* up to me," Rosie says. "Mom said."

I have to bite my lip for a second. "Right. So

what color do you want? It's your room too, you know. Besides, I have my workshop, so I guess . . ." I swallow hard. "It might be more your room than mine."

She turns to the display. "Any color?" she asks, wrinkling her forehead.

I squeeze my eyes shut and take a deep breath. "What do you want to see in the morning?" I ask, nudging her with my elbow. "What do you want to think about as soon as you wake up every day?"

She smiles at me then, her eyes shining. "Fairy wings," she breathes.

Fairy wings? I almost scream the words, but I force myself to keep a straight face and nod. "That sounds like you."

Slowly, carefully, Rosie runs her finger along the colors on the lightest side of the cards, all the way down the display.

My chest starts to ache. She'll pick a shade of *nothing*, I know it—something light and wispy and barely there.

And I could stop her! Sisters look out for each other, don't they? It's for her own good.

But I don't. I don't do anything . . . until her finger stops on a card.

A pink one.

I grit my teeth, slip my beautiful color back into its slot, and pick up Rosie's card. "This one?" I ask.

She crinkles her forehead. "It does look like fairy wings," she says.

It also looks like the cupcake Aiden wouldn't eat. It looks like canopy beds and tea parties and that stupid cleaning set grandma gave me for my birthday before she found out I would never, ever clean anything I didn't have to.

"Would it look good in our room?" she asks.

Our room.

Rosie always calls it that.

I hand her the card. "Let's find out."

"But what if it's not the right one?"

"It's right if it's the one you want."

Mom rounds the corner, a big bag of grass seed in her arms. "Ready?"

Rosie bounces on her toes. "Ready!"

I pat her on the back, then turn and head into the next aisle so she won't see my face.

I let my hands drift over the rack of hammers and pliers and wrenches, thinking of that perfect shade of starry sky that I won't get to see every day, feeling every drop of that color leaking out my toes.

But right when I'm almost empty, I feel something else start trickling in through the top of my head, filling me back up, like a bicycle tire being pumped full of air.

I feel a little bit proud of myself. For doing nothing at all.

I might not be a superhero, but I'm Rosie's hero.

I hope I deserve to be.

I turn back down the main aisle. Because I still have quarters in my pocket, and I know what to do with them now.

21

On Sunday afternoon, Rosie and I hang out in my workshop while Mom and Dad start painting our room. We drag blankets and pillows in here so we can have a sleepover tonight while the paint dries. I think we should do it again when Sofía comes over next Friday, because who says you can't have a sleepover with your best friend *and* your sister?

For now, I try to push away the thought of all that pink going up on the walls.

I'll be a good sport about it. I will.

But not any sooner than I have to be.

Rosie and I make a big nest of softness in the middle of the workshop floor. She sets Pink Pony on the pillow next to her, sets Raymond on the pillow next to me, then lies down on her stomach to color. She hums for a while, her feet kicked up in the air, while I smooth out my hero poster and tape it back onto the wall.

I stand back and take a look. It's still blank

inside, the rainbow spreading out from that hollow figure in the center. But maybe that doesn't mean there's nobody there.

Maybe it means it could be anybody. Even an everyday kid like me.

I'm starting to smell the paint now, but I try not to think about it while I rummage around in my bins. It only takes a minute to find what I'm looking for and put the whole thing together. "Hey, Rosie," I say when I'm finished.

"Hmm?"

"Do you know what this is?"

She looks up at the Ring, dangling from a rainbow shoelace.

"Your good-luck charm," she says.

"Nope." I plop down in front of her, pull down my T-shirt, and show her the Rainbow Ring that's hanging around my neck again.

Rosie looks from one to the other. "Why do you have two of them?"

"Because one of them is yours."

She sits all the way up. "Mine?" The ring I bought at the hardware store is so shiny and new that it catches the light and flashes in midair as it spins. "What is it?" Rosie asks.

For a second, I want to say it's a talisman—a magical charm that activates your powers and makes you better than you were before.

But it doesn't. It doesn't have to.

So I say, "It's a washer."

Rosie squints at me. "What does it wash?"

"It doesn't wash anything," I reply. "It helps hold things together. Not by itself, though. It works with other pieces. If they stick together, they're even stronger. Like you and me. You know why?"

Her eyes light up. "Why?"

"Because we're sisters."

"Friends, too?" she asks quietly.

I smile. "Friends, too." The Rainbow Ring shines and twirls between us. I open up the shoelace and lean toward her. Rosie bows her head, and I put it on her like a medal. She lifts it off her chest and gazes down at it.

Mom pokes her head in the door. "We finished the first wall," she says. "Want to come take a look?"

Rosie jumps up. "Yes!" She goes flying past Mom and thumps down the hall. In a few seconds, I hear her squeal.

I sigh and get to my feet.

Mom ruffles my hair. "Thanks for being such a good sport about this."

I nod and square my shoulders.

The plasticky smell of the paint gets stronger with each step. I can almost feel myself breathing in the pink air, filling up on it, whether I want to or not. I keep my head down, waiting until the very last second to look.

At least it's not gray anymore, I tell myself. *At least it's not beige or white.*

I take a deep breath and step into the room.

Holy hot dog!

"Do you like it?" Rosie asks.

I stand there blinking. This isn't the color she showed me in the store. It isn't the color I wanted, either. It's a gauzy glow of bluish purple. It's my color but softer, like the sun is shining through it.

"It isn't pink," I say.

"Nuh-uh," Rosie says.

"Why isn't it pink?"

"It's not just my room," she says. "It's ours."

"But—" I'm stuttering now. "You wanted pink," I manage finally. "You *love* pink."

"I love you more." She squeezes my hand. "And sisters look out for each other."

I almost sob. I had to practically force myself to do the nice thing, the generous thing. Why is it so easy for her?

"But it was your pick," I say, blinking back tears. "Do you even like it?"

"I love it!" She jumps up and down, clapping. "It looks like fairy wings!"

I breathe a sigh of relief, hook my arm around her neck, and kiss the top her head.

She loves it. She couldn't fake it if she didn't. Because when Rosie loves something, she loves it with her whole heart. Pink Pony. Fairy wing purple. Me.

It's like her superpower.

I hope someday I have one like it.

Mom and Dad let us help finish painting. Mom uses a brush to outline the edges, nice and neat. Dad shows us how to use big rollers to color inside the lines, then follows behind us to clean up splatters and smooth out places where the paint is uneven.

Which is kind of a lot, because I keep making zigzags with my roller instead of filling up the wall.

When we're finished, we stand back and look at the whole room.

It's a good color. I'm not gonna lie: It doesn't make me feel like I've been dunked in purple. But I do feel like I've been sprinkled with it, like cinnamon sugar on toast, or that powdery snow that blows off the trees and makes the ground look brand-new.

I bet when I wake up in the morning, it will make me think of Rosie—how she's her own person, and not just my sidekick. How sometimes she gets her way, sometimes I get mine, and sometimes we both do. Maybe I'll remember how lucky I am to have a sister like her.

Well, probably not *every* morning.

"How about we get some ice cream while the paint dries?" Mom says when we put down our rollers. "We can stop for Eli on the way."

"Yes!" Rosie and I both shout and jump up and down.

"The bikes are ready," Dad says.

But I have a better idea.

When we get outside, I drag my office chair from around back, park it at the top of the driveway, and ride the short slope down to the sidewalk.

Dad laughs.

"Where on earth did that thing come from?" Mom asks.

I spin myself around. "Isn't it great? We can ride it to the scoop shop!"

Rosie sighs. "You want me to push you all the way there?"

"Nope." I stand up. "It's your turn."

She looks up at me, her eyes wide. "Really?"

I grin and wave toward the seat. Rosie hops on, and I spin her around until she giggles and squeals and begs me to stop. Then I start rolling her down the sidewalk. Mom and Dad follow behind, hand in hand in their paint-splattered clothes.

"Are you ready?" I ask.

"Ready!" She grabs the bottom of the seat.

I put my head down, bracing my arms against the back of the chair.

Then we take off flying.

Acknowledgments

It was such a joy to write about Meena again! Thank you to Simon & Schuster Books for Young Readers for giving me the opportunity. The whole team there is fabulous, but I was fortunate to work closely with senior editor Krista Vitola and associate editor Catherine Laudone. Thank you both for the love and labor you poured into this story. I'm also grateful to my agent, Emily Mitchell, who pulled Meena out of the slush pile and who has acted as my sounding board and advocate ever since. I'm so glad to have you in my corner!

Thank you to Tom Daly for creating a book design that is as fun and exuberant as Meena, and to the amazing Mina Price for stepping in as illustrator. As soon as I saw samples of your work, I knew I was in good hands.

I credit my friends and allies in the Wisconsin chapter of SCBWI for showing me that writing children's books is possible, important, and a whole lot of fun. I'm particularly grateful to the authors who answered impertinent questions during my debut year: Jane Kelley, Sandy Brehl, Liza M. Weimer, and Valerie Biel. My critique group also came through for me, as always. This book is better for the keen eyes and honesty of Moy Ahmad, Jeff Schill, J. Mercer, Nancy McConnell, Vicki Hubert Menuge, and Jenn Van Haaften. I owe a debt of gratitude to my sensitivity readers as well: Laura Pérez-Hametta and Julio Andrade.

To the friends and family who have never stopped rooting for me, thank you. I'm grateful to my parents, Jerome and Carolyn Manternach, and to everyone who hit the streets to sing my praises, especially Jeremy and Anna Johnson Manternach, Brian and Erika Edberg Manternach, and Kathy and Sean Culbertson. Thank you most of all to my husband, Brian Zanin. I can't imagine a career path more unpredictable than publishing, but with you at my side, I always feel like I'm on solid ground. Thanks also to my children, Mara and Amelia, for letting me borrow from your lives yet again. You are my Inspiration!

Finally, I'd like to thank the parents, teachers, librarians, and bookstore staff who have welcomed me into your worlds and onto your shelves. Above all, thank you to my readers. The best part of this journey has been connecting with you!

TURN THE PAGE
FOR A SNEAK PEEK AT
MEENA LOST AND FOUND

KARLA MANTERNACH

meena
LOST AND FOUND

Our milk jug igloo is the perfect spot for club meetings.

I drop to my knees and crawl inside. It's cool and wet today, but it's cozy and dry in here. Milk lids dot the walls in rainbow colors—blue for skim, green for low fat, and red for whole. We even have orange, which you only get when you buy milk jugs full of juice!

The only color that's missing is pink for strawberry milk. I feel a twinge in my stomach every time I notice. Sofía would have brought those jugs, but we were in a fight when we built the igloo, so I didn't invite her.

I call through the doorway, "Are you two coming?"

Eli crawls in and sits across from me, his knees muddy. "She's checking for eggs again," he says with a grin.

I groan. Sofía loves Eli's chickens. She's always watching them peck at their feathers or opening the little drawers of the coop to look for eggs. I'm about to call her again when I stop.

Give her a minute, I tell myself.

I've been Sofía's best friend since kindergarten, but…well, I haven't always been very good at it. Sometimes I forget to give her a turn or listen to her ideas. A few times I've stopped talking to her because I was mad or hurt. I do listen when she moans about getting a word wrong on her spelling test. I put up with the way she smoothes out the blankets after I sit on her bed. She also has a thing about wearing black socks with her navy blue sneakers, and I've never once said anything about it.

But Sofía has been a much better friend to me. She helps me collect beautiful trash. She trades lunch food with me to make sure I get every color of the rainbow. And this year, when I started having seizures, and none of the other kids would come near me, Sofía stayed right by my side.

I take a big breath and make myself wait. It's her club, too, even if it is my turn to be president.

When she finally crawls in, I scooch back against the wall, pick up our big metal spoon, and clang it against the floor. "Order! Order! The Finders Keepers Club is now in session! Vice

President Eli, what's first on our agenda?"

"Snacks. I brought popcorn." He rattles the bag in his hand and empties it onto the floorboards in the middle of our circle.

"I brought chicles," Sofía says, reaching into her pocket. The little rectangles click as she drops them into the pile. Technically, they aren't a snack, since you can't swallow gum, but they come in cool flavors like cough drop and black jelly bean.

I reach into the front pocket of my tie-dyed hoodie. "I brought animal crackers." I open the little box, dump it onto the floor, and scoop up a handful.

"Next is savings," Eli says.

I crunch on my snack and turn to Sofía. "Madam Treasurer, how much money have we found?"

She peeks inside the spare jug we use for a bank. "Nine cents since we started the club. Four pennies and a nickel."

We nod at each other, impressed. Eli was the one who spotted the nickel two weeks ago, but I found three of the pennies myself, which is the most coins, even if it isn't worth the most.

Not that it's a contest or anything.

I swallow and pick up two cinnamon chicles.

My mouth feels spicy as I start to chew.

"Treasures next," Eli says. "I'll go first." He opens the little baggie in his lap and holds up a limp yellow leaf.

"It looks like a fan," Sofía says.

"That's because it's from a Gingko tree." He passes it around then holds up an acorn.

"What's so great about that?" I ask. "They're all over."

"But the top is still attached," he says. "Usually they come apart before you find them."

I nod. "Okay, cool. What's your third thing?"

He reaches into his bag again and pulls out two pinecones that are fused together at the top.

"Nice," Sofía says, tracing one with her finger.

"Your turn," he says to her when he's put his collection away. "What'd you find this week?"

Sofía lights up and opens her worn-out bird book. She doesn't like finding treasures the way Eli and I do, but she's always looking for the birds that are listed in her book, so we decided that could count as her collection. "I saw a blue jay this morning," she says, holding up a picture.

I try to seem excited, but I'm not gonna lie. I was kind of hoping for an ostrich.

"What was it doing?" Eli asks sharply.

Sofía blinks. "Just sitting there."

He crosses his arms. "Blue jays are mean, you know. They attack other birds."

"They're so pretty, though." She fingers the edge of the page. "Their feathers look like a stained glass window."

Eli's face softens. "What else did you see?"

"A lot more robins this week," she says, turning pages. "And I didn't see it, but I heard a red-winged blackbird."

"I saw a junco yesterday," Eli says.

"Really?"

"The squirrels scared him off, though. They can't get into my feeder, but they chase away the birds that eat from the ground." He brightens. "Wanna hear me do a squirrel?"

Oh, no. If Eli gets started with his sound effects, I might never get a turn. He stretches his mouth wide and makes a scratchy sound in the back of this throat. "Ack-ack-ack!"

Sofía beams at him. "You sound just like one!"

Eli smiles, his ears going pink.

I sigh and start twisting the strings of my hoodie.

I think Sofía notices, though, because she bumps her shoulder against mine and says, "What did you find this week?"

Finally!

I sit up straighter. Not to brag, but I'd say my trash collection is the highlight of our meetings. I reach into my pocket and pull out a scraped-up doll head with rainbow streaks in her hair. "I found this in a parking lot," I say, "but I added the highlights myself. And check this out!" I open my hand to show them an oval sunglass lens that looks like a mirror. Last but not least, I pull out my best find of the week: a red plastic comb with so many missing teeth that—

"It looks like the letter E!" Sofía says.

I hand it to Eli. "Just two more letters, and I'll be able to write your name in trash."

He laughs and looks it over.

"I have something else for the agenda," I say.

He passes the comb to Sofía. "What?"

"Our club needs a project."

"We have a project," Sofía says. "We collect treasures."

"We'll keep doing that, but we need something bigger. I was thinking…" I lean in closer. "You know how you see some stores and restaurants all over, no matter how far you go from home?"

They nod.

"I think our club should be like that."

"Like a chain?" Eli asks.

"Why not?" I ask. "This could be our main headquarters, and we could open clubhouses all over town—all over the world, even. And when people land on Mars, we could build the first clubhouse there!"

Eli raises his eyebrows at me. "You want to build a clubhouse on another planet?"

"We'll open a new one in town first."

"Where?" Sofía asks.

"At your place." I loop my pinky through her friendship bracelet. "You should get the next clubhouse since you didn't get to help build this one. All those in favor?" I put my hand in the air.

They shrug at each other and raise their hands.

"Yes!" I'm so happy that I throw my arms out, lean back against the wall and—

I'm falling!

The jugs squeak as the wall shifts behind me. Sofía grabs my arm and pulls me up as the dome caves in. "Don't let it fall," I cry, pushing against the ceiling. Eli and Sofía use their hands to brace it.

The squeaking stops. I hold my breath. We stare at each other with big eyes.

"What do we do?" Sofía asks.

Slowly, I ease my hands away. The ceiling sags a little more. "Wait here," I say, scrambling out the door. The igloo slumps at the top now and is leaning to one side.

In a minute, I crawl back in with an umbrella from the hall closet.

"What are you gonna do with that?" Eli asks.

"Open it. But I don't want to hit you in the face. On the count of three, you hit the floor. Ready? One, two—"

Eli and Sofía duck. I hit the release. The ceiling starts to droop, but the umbrella opens, catches it, and lifts it away from us.

We all let out a big breath.

"That was close," I say. It looks like a circus tent in here now with the striped umbrella above us.

"You can't hold it forever," Sofía says.

"I'll get something to prop it up," Eli says. He crawls out and comes back with a big white bucket. When he sets it in the middle of the igloo, I carefully rest the handle of the umbrella on the lid. When I'm pretty sure it's steady, I let go. The umbrella balances on the bucket and holds up the dome. We crawl out to check for damage.

The igloo is lopsided now, and the wall has a big bulge in it that wasn't there before. But at least it's still in one piece. I grin at them. "Good as new!"

Eli stares at me. "Are you serious?"

"If you tilt your head, you can't even tell how crooked it is. Try it."

He does, but he still says, "I don't think that'll last."

"Sure it will."

There's a gust of wind, and the dome of jugs sways. I jump forward and throw out my arms, like maybe hugging the whole igloo would help. The wind dies down and the igloo goes still again.

I cringe. "It'll be okay, right?"

Eli and Sofía look at each other.

"I know," I say. "Why don't we—"

Ack-ack-ack!

Eli holds up a hand. "Shhh," he says, turning toward the yard.

Sofía and I freeze. For a minute, I don't hear anything except the soft clucking of the chickens behind us. Then the sound comes again.

Ack-ack-ack!

"The squirrel!" Eli clambers down the porch steps with a loud bellow, waving his arms over his head. Sofía and I chase after him in time to see birds scattering into the air and something zipping away from the feeder. Sofía gasps as it streaks though the yard and disappears into the brush.

"What was that?" I ask. It didn't look like a squirrel. It had spots—white and black and orange.

"I don't know." Eli says. "Maybe a rabbit?"

Sofía starts moving toward the brush and stops.

I go to stand next to her. "What's the matter?" I ask, following her gaze. "What are you looking at?"

"That wasn't a rabbit," she says. She turns to us then, her eyes wide. "I think it was Oriol."

O riol?" I ask. "What would he be doing here?"
Sofía hurries toward the brush and starts calling in a singsong. "Oriol! Oriol!"

We fan out to look. Eli makes a clicking sound with his mouth. I try calling, "Here, kitty, kitty!" Sofía's cat has never come to me before, and I don't know why he'd start now, but I feel like I should do something to help.

After a few minutes, we still haven't found him. "Are you sure it was him?" Eli asks. "I've never seen him in our yard before."

"Maybe not," Sofía says. She sounds doubtful.

"Well, if it was," I say, "he's probably back home by now anyway."

I don't see what the big deal is. Oriol is always wandering around Sofía's yard. Who cares if he's gone a few blocks farther?

I glance back at the porch. "We should check on the igloo," I say. "I bet if we fill it up with balloons it won't fall. Or we could build some kind of frame for it. Or what if we hung something from the porch ceiling to hold it up?"

Eli shrugs, but Sofía doesn't answer. She just stands there, squinting into the brush.

I shift from one foot to the other. It took months to pull enough jugs out of the neighborhood recycling bins to build our igloo. And it was worth it! It turned out even better than I imagined! I can't let anything to happen to it now.

But Sofía almost always goes along with whatever I want. For a long time I figured it was because I had the best ideas. But I think maybe sometimes I forget to ask.

I guess the igloo is okay. I hope.

"Would you rather go to your house?" I ask. "Make sure Oriol is there?"

Sofía looks at me. "You don't mind?"

I stuff my hands into my front pocket and cross my fingers. Technically, I'm about to tell a tiny lie, and I don't want it to count. "I don't mind."

She takes a big breath and nods.

I unclip the walkie talkie from the waistband of my pants and press the talk button. "Big Zee to

Zee Money. Come in, Zee Money, over."

There's a pause, then my dad's voice crackles through the speaker. "Zee Money here. Go ahead, over."

"Zookeeper and I are headed to the Flamingo's. Do you copy, over?"

"I copy, Big Zee. Stick together, and holler when you get there, over."

"Roger that, Zee Money. Over and out."

I hook the walkie talkie back onto my pants. I get to go a lot more places on my own since I started using it. I got the idea from those CB radio things that truck drivers use in videos. Mom and Dad won't let me have my own phone, but at least this makes me feel like a trucker!

Eli calls through the back door to tell Aunt Kathy where we're going, then we pocket our treasures and head for Sofía's. The world's a lot more colorful now that it's spring. The grass is turning green, and the tulips are blooming—red and purple and yellow. It rained this morning, and it's still cold enough that I pull my hands into the sleeves of my sweatshirt as we walk.

Eli runs ahead to rescue earthworms that are stranded on the sidewalk. Sofía trails behind, looking for birds. I stoop down and pick up a worm that Eli missed. Then I check the curb for interesting trash.

I find most of my treasures after the garbage truck comes by on Wednesdays. It has mechanical arms that pick up the bins and dump them into the back. Sometimes the wind catches little bits of trash as they're falling. It sends them flying around the streets until somebody picks them up again.

Usually that somebody is me. I'm not exactly a tidy-up-after-myself kind of a kid, but I do keep this neighborhood pretty clean.

A few houses from Sofía's, I hit the trash jackpot.

Someone put a ton of cool stuff on the curb: a planter with a big crack in it, a rake with a broken handle, and a lawn chair that's turned inside out. There's even a rusted-out wagon. It's all just sitting there with a sign that says FREE, one of my favorite words in the world.

"Look at this," I say when Sofía catches up to me. "Why are people getting rid of so much great stuff lately?"

She shrugs. "Spring cleaning?"

I give her a funny look. Why would anybody clean when it's finally nice outside? Or ever?

I gaze at that wonderful pile of trash. If I had a pickup truck, I'd take it all. I'd drive around on bulk trash day, talking to other truckers on my CB radio and hauling away the cool stuff people chucked onto the curb.

Hang on.

My eyes zoom in on the wagon. The metal bottom is flaky with rust, and when I pull it out of the pile, one of the wheels screeches. But it's big enough for me to set the lawn chair across the back and load the planter and the rake on top. It's all mine now!

"What are you gonna do with that?" Sofía asks.

"Something awesome." I haul my wagon down the sidewalk, the wheel squealing as my brain sparks with ideas. "Maybe we'll use it to make our new clubhouse!"

She looks at me. "Don't you want to use milk jugs?"

"We can build with whatever we want. That way, every location will be one of a kind!" I get a zillion Inspirations thinking about it— a wall of lawn chair webbing, upside-down flower pots turned into seats, pillars made out of old garden tools!

Then I catch myself. Sofía should get to pick.

We don't exactly have the same style. She likes to make things pretty. I like to make things that are big and colorful. But I don't want to take over and get her to do what I want like usual. This time, I'll collect supplies so she can decide. She has good ideas of her own, and it'll be her clubhouse, after all. "What do you think it should look like?" I ask.

She blinks. "Me?"

"Sure," I say. "If we work together, this could be the best thing we ever made."

"Michi, michi, michi!"

Sofía straightens at the sound of a voice coming from up ahead. Her mom is in their front yard, rummaging through the tulips along the house. Her dad is nearby, checking under some bushes.

"Mamá?" Sofía runs up to her. I catch up with Eli and park the wagon by the front steps. For a minute, they talk together in Spanish, then Sofía looks over her shoulder at us. "Oriol's gone," she says.

Her dad pats her on the back. "Don't worry, mija. He's never missing for long."

It's funny to see Sofía's dad in gym shorts and flip flops. Usually, I only see him in brown overalls and rubber boots. But the family he worked for sold their farm a little while ago, and I guess he's still looking for another job.

"We'll go ask the neighbors to keep an eye out for him," her dad says.

Sofía sighs. "Okay."

He says something to her mom in Spanish, and they head next door.

"What happened?" Eli asks.

Sofía rolls her eyes. "Oriol ran after a rabbit."

Eli looks worried, but I bet he's thinking about the rabbit, not Oriol. "Don't you keep him in the house?" he asks.

"We used to, but he always wanted to go out, so my dad put a flap on the door. He usually stays in the yard." She sighs again.

"He used to be a stray, right?" Eli asks. "Maybe he misses hunting."

She laughs. "Well, he shouldn't. He isn't any good at it. He's always chasing the birds, but he never catches any."

Eli looks relieved at that. "Then he'll probably come back when he's hungry."

Sofía frowns. "I hate it when he runs off."

"I'm sure he's fine," I say. "He probably just went exploring."

She bites her lip and looks away.

I glance at Eli.

Here's the thing Sofía doesn't know about Oriol.

I'm not exactly his biggest fan.

I mean, he's handsome and all—sort of sleek and kingly, snowy white with black and orange spots all over. But he isn't even soft. He's actually kind of bristly. He's got this pinchy-looking face, too, and all he does is chase the birds and lie around licking himself clean. Every time I pet him, I think about all that licking and feel like I've got cat spit on my hands.

I don't know what Sofía sees in him.

But I know she loves him. A lot. So I don't really have to ask what she wants to do now, because I already know.

"You want us to help you look for him?"

She perks up at that, then lets her shoulders slump. "That's okay. I'm sure he's fine."

I nudge her with my elbow. "Come on, it'll be fun. We can even make it a game!"

"What kind of game?" asks Eli.

"A contest." I grin. "The first one to find Oriol wins."